Restored

H. L. Wegley

Romantic Suspense

ISBN-13: 978-1-7344890-3-3
ISBN-10: 1734489030

Also available in eBook publication

OTHER BOOKS BY H. L. WEGLEY

Against All Enemies Series
1 Voice in the Wilderness
2 Voice of Freedom
3 Chasing Freedom

Pure Genius Series
1 Hide and Seek
2 On the Pineapple Express
3 Moon over Maalaea Bay
4 Triple Threat

Witness Protection Series
1 No Safe Place
2 No True Justice
3 No Turning Back

Stand-Alone Books
Virtuality
The Janus Journals
Slanted

Riven Republic Series
1 Riven
2 Resisting
3 Restored

DEDICATION

Restored is dedicated to the preachers in the pulpits of our churches who are faithfully calling our nation to repentance and asking God to awaken us and turn us as a nation back to the Him and the faith that our founders relied on when they prepared the United States of America to take its place among the self-governing nations of the world.

CONTENTS

ACKNOWLEDGMENTS

Thanks to my wife, Babe, for listening to me read two drafts of the manuscript and catching the logical errors.

Thanks again, Gail Ostheller, for proofing this novel and catching mistakes my deteriorating vision can't seem to spot these days.

A big thank you to Dr. Eddie L. Hyatt for writing *1726: The Year that Defined America.*

https://www.amazon.com/1726-Year-that-Defined-America/dp/1888435402/

Dr. Hyatt's book illustrated through historical events how movements of God across our nation at critical times have prepared us for what was to come—e.g. self-government in 1776, the Civil War bringing an end to slavery in America, and the Jesus Movement at a time when no-fault divorce coupled with expanded welfare was wreaking havoc on our families and God was being shoved out of the national conversation.

And thanks to our Lord for helping me, after a nine-month hiatus, to finish this story. I hope He finds it pleasing and honoring to Him.

CAST OF CHARACTERS

Radley Baker – a vet, a half Modoc, and a pilot now serving in the Eastern Oregon militia. Radley is a short, muscular man who bench-presses well over 400 pounds.

Shauna Jackson – Kate's roommate and best friend since college is a beautiful, petite African American woman who has her eye on Radley Baker, but her sharp tongue gets in the way.

Colonel David Craig – a recently retired Ranger commander and a national hero, age 45. He starred in *Voice in the Wilderness* and *Voice of Freedom*.

Susan O'Connell – the original owner of Crooked River Espresso in Terrebonne. She's 37, a patriotic American, a team builder, and an admirer of David Craig.

Zach Tanner – hero of *Riven*, a radio show host, patriotic American and a Christian.

Kate Alexander – heroine of *Riven*, a new Christian, niece of the leftist Oregon governor, Sandra Harper, whom Kate wants to lead from her Marxist roots to Bible-based conservatism.

Jeff and Allie Jacobs – hero and heroine from *Chasing Freedom*. Jeff was a world class decathlete and Allie an international scholarship student from Mexico. They have a seven-year-old daughter, **Lori**.

Lex and Gemma James – hero and heroine of *No True Justice*. Both are investigative journalists. They adopted high-IQ, nine-year-old twins, **Josh and Caleb**.

KC and Brock Daniels – hero and heroine of *Voice in the Wilderness*. KC knows computers, and has gained a reputation as a hacker, and Brock is an athlete and a Christian apologist with a huge blog following. Their son **Benjamin** is ten and very bright like his mom and dad.

Drew and Beth West – hero and heroine of *No Turning Back*. They own a horse ranch. Drew knows weapons and martial arts. **Beth**, who claimed asylum after a drug cartel killed her family in Mexico, has an MBA. Their son **Peter** is four.

Steve and Julia Bancroft – hero and heroine of *Voice of Freedom*. Steve is an ex-Army Ranger, Craig's weapons sergeant. Julia inherited her grandparents' mansion on Crooked River Ranch, which she uses to host meetings and provide a temporary home for those in transition. **Itzy** (Itzell), their adopted daughter from Guatemala, is 19. She is Mayan.

Hunter and AJ Jones – hero and heroine from *Slanted.* Hunter is a big data analyst. AJ is a barista. Their adopted daughter **Sam** (Samantha) is 13 going on 18 and is a handful.

Oregon Governor Sandra Harper – initially an antagonist who heads the leftist politicians in Oregon. She loves her niece, Kate, and wants to bring her back home to her roots in the most powerful political family in the state. But Sandra's thinking is changing in many subtle ways.

President Wendell Walker – the main antagonist of the *Riven Republic Series*, a far-left radical who wants to unify the nation by force under his tyrannical leadership.

Secretary of Defense William Richards – a cabinet member and confidant of President Walker who often gives the president sound advice that is not always accepted.

Laura Alexander – Kate's mother and the little sister of Governor Sandra Harper. Laura is a member of the left-wing political society in Oregon.

Major Nicholas Deke – Former military special ops officer, now a spy planted in Oregon by President Walker. He is the brother of Captain Albert Deke who was shot and killed nine years earlier by Julia Bancroft (Weiss).

Henderson – member of Major Deke's black ops team

Babak – another member of Major Deke's black ops team

Tige Martin (scar face) – leader of black ops team sent to Salem, Oregon by President Wendell Walker to capture the governor.

Dietrich – a member of Martin's team

Finley – another member of Martin's team

Colonel Blackford – Stryker Brigade commander

Colonel Whittingham – commander of the 173rd Fighter Wing at Kingsley AFB, Klamath Falls, Oregon

Bob Daggett – an older member of the militia who's a Cessna pilot.

Airman Kathy Gore – a patriotic young woman who attempts to help the militia

Then God saw their works, that they turned from their evil way; and God relented from the disaster that He had said He would bring upon them...
(Jonah 3:10 NKJV)

Prologue

A recap of Riven and Resisting

The United States is fragmenting along geopolitical lines, blue against red, left against right. The nation's production threatens to grind down to a halt as *de facto* secession informally splits the union, threatening the fragile systems that form the nation's lifelines.

Nearly a month ago, conservative radio talk show host, Zach Tanner, advised his audience to leave Western Oregon and congregate in Eastern Oregon to avoid martial law which was declared by leftist governor Sandra Harper to quell the violence in Salem and the Portland area.

Sandra Harper's niece, Kate Alexander, is a new Christian who finds herself at odds with the atheistic aunt who used to be closer to her than Kate's own mother. Kate manages to escape both the martial law and the BOLO her aunt put out for her, and she hitches a ride to Terrebonne, Oregon, where she buys, from Susan O'Connell, Crooked River Espresso, a coffee drive-through along Highway 97.

There Kate meets the DJ she's been listening to, Zach Tanner, and they join forces with an incredible group of people living on and around Crooked River Ranch. Kate and Zach find a strong bond forming between them and there is a budding romance.

In a meeting at the Ranch Chapel, the group from Crooked River Ranch organizes a militia. David Craig, retired Army Ranger commander, heads that effort. Zach Tanner builds a radio station to broadcast to the other red states and red areas across the nation. They hope to organize and help each other defend themselves against the neo-Marxist president while they formulate a plan to unify the nation.

President Wendell Walker, a leftist, wants to unify the fragmenting nation by force—martial law, threats, intimidation of governors, and by using the military to wipe out any insurgents. However, the military is also fragmenting, and Walker cannot depend on all of the officers to carry out his commands. And if he pushes too hard, the infrastructure of the nation will fracture, leaving Walker the president of a failed state.

The Central Oregon Militia is a thorn in the president's side, and he wants to make them an example to all the other potential insurgents. When the militia leader, Craig, confronts Sandra Harper, who has kidnapped Kate to take her home and "fix her," Walker thinks he has a chance to kill them all at the same time and take over Oregon himself by using succession to place a strong Walker supporter in the governor's office. But Kate, the militia members, and an injured Governor Harper survive Walker's brutal attack.

Injured and nearly killed, Harper has an epiphany. She cannot trust the president. The other blue state governors will now not trust her nor will the red state governors. She's isolated, alone, and President Walker wants her killed before she can tell the world about his attempted murder of a governor.

Kate accompanies her injured aunt back to Salem, where Governor Harper, with Kate's influence, decides to flip Oregon from blue to red, though she knows this will create a lot of enemies in the state government, and it will take work to get the conservatives, especially the Oregon Guard, to trust her.

Since both the state of Oregon and Sandra Harper are Walker's targets, she asks militia commander, David Craig, to meet with her to work out a joint defense plan for Oregon. Craig agrees but has not yet met with Harper.

Zach Tanner has spent every spare moment with Kate, and though these are tumultuous times, he proposes to her. She accepts on the condition that Zach courts her until there is a lull in the fighting so they can marry.

The United States is now *Riven*. The story continues as red areas and red states are actively *Resisting* the increasingly tyrannical federal government of President Wendell Walker.

In *Resisting*, after flipping Oregon from Blue to Red, Governor Harper formed a compact with the militia to jointly protect Oregon from the now hostile President Walker. He takes steps immediately to try to kill the militia leaders as they fly to meet with Governor Harper.

When Walker fails to eliminate the militia leaders, he sends a spy and begins planning for a larger-scale assault and an assassination attempt on Governor Harper to bring a Walker loyalist to the governorship of Oregon.

President Walker attempts to take out the radio voice of the militia, Zach Tanner, via an Apache attack on the Bancroft mansion where Zach is staying. But the genius of the twins, Josh and Caleb, with help from their cousin, Benjamin, take down the Apache using a racing drone.

When Susan tries to sacrifice her life to save everyone at the Bancroft house, David Craig senses that his admiration for Susan is morphing into deeper feelings, feelings that must be set aside during this time of warfare.

Fearful of President Walker's next attempt to retaliate, Craig uses KC Daniels' hacking experience to learn of Walker's plans, an attack on the militia leaders and their families using two Apache attack helicopters, two JLTVs, and one hundred troops deployed by Chinook helicopters all under command of Colonel Towry from JBLM (Joint Base Lewis-McChord) in Tacoma, Washington.

Craig hides the militia leaders and their families in the Skylight Cave. Airman Gore, a patriotic young woman working in the Western Air Defense Headquarters, warns Craig of the attack and notifies the Oregon Air Guard, which takes down the Apaches.

The hiding place in the cave is compromised by Deke. This forces the families to flee in the night to a rendezvous point at Clear Lake. Craig devises a plan to neutralize and capture the JLTVs, but Craig and Susan are last to leave the cave and are captured by Deke and his men. Craig is wounded, but Susan's cleverness and courage help the two escape.

Deke's men find the women, kids, and the other non-warfighters at Clear Lake. He tries to take them into custody, but a spunky, brave Shauna Jackson bluffs them to a stalemate and David Craig arrives to help her turn a stand-off into a victory resulting in the capture of Deke's black ops team.

When the troops under Colonel Towry arrive a short time later, the militia, with their confiscated JLTVs and help from Governor Harper's Oregon Guard, defeat the JBLM troops in hardly more than sixty seconds, using a volley of Hellfire Missiles and rifle fire. The three boys, Josh, Caleb, and their cousin Benjamin, play a significant role too.

Back at Crooked River Ranch, for the first time, Craig reveals his true feelings for Susan. Then he calls a meeting of the militia leaders to prepare for battle, because a humiliated Wendell Walker will retaliate with the strongest force he can muster. And he won't wait long to attack.

Chapter 1

July 25, 2:30 p.m., Terrebonne, Oregon

Radley Baker made the turn onto NW 43rd and shoved the accelerator to the floor.

The 700-horsepower engine under the hood of his Trackhawk sent the big SUV surging ahead of the motorcycle that had been glued to his rear bumper since he turned off from Highway 97 at Terrebonne.

Why was someone following him? Was President Walker trying to pick off the Central Oregon Militia one-by-one and he was the first victim?

Baker glanced down at his M4 riding shotgun beside him.

Nah.

He didn't need the gun. Baker had 700 horsepower and outweighed the bike and rider by at least two-and-a-half tons. He could run over them if it came to that.

The road ran straight for the next mile, but the straightaway ended in sweeping S-curves. Maybe he could shake the dude on the bike before the curves.

Baker punched the gas pedal and accelerated to a hundred miles-per-hour before he braked, preparing for the curves.

The motorcycle caught up to him. From the looks and the acceleration of the Honda racing bike, it could have passed him had the rider been foolhardy enough to try.

He slowed and took the curves at a sane speed.

Baker had frequently been accused of being a dare devil, but that would not be the case tonight.

Five miles ahead, Shauna Jackson, AKA Munchkin, the cutest little spitfire on this side of the mountains, waited for him, and this was one date Baker would not miss, not even for the thrill of outracing a—what was that bike on his tail? A Honda Fireblade?

Thoughts of a Fireblade brought a number to mind. Top end, 186 miles-per-hour.

Hey, dude. If you want to see Munchkin, don't race the bike.

For once the annoying voice inside had offered some sound advice. His Trackhawk had power, but that motorcycle was designed for speed.

Baker slowed and prepared to take the ninety-degree turn onto Northwest Chinook Drive.

The bike pulled into the left lane and accelerated until he was looking into the faceplate of the biker's helmet. The tinted face shield hid the face behind it.

The tingling climbing Baker's spine sent his right hand reaching for his M4. But there was no weapon in the biker's hand.

The biker nodded at him then fell in behind his Trackhawk.

Baker negotiated the right-angle turn.

He'd just been checked out and approved by some dude on a racing bike, whatever that meant.

The protective riding suit hid the biker's body, but after a close-up look, that was not a guy straddling the Fireblade.

A woman riding a lightning-fast racing bike? That was unusual to say the least. Who was she and what did she want?

His curiosity could wait the four remaining miles to Julia's and Steve's house where Shauna was staying. Either the biker would follow him to the house or turn down the hill to the golf course and restaurants.

After the checkout and approving nod, his gut said the bike would follow him.

Five minutes later, Baker turned in to the circle drive at the Bancrofts' mansion.

David Craig's Jeep and Zach Tanner's truck were parked ahead of him.

The militia commander and their talk show host had come. Was there a militia meeting going on? No one told him about it.

Behind him, the bike braked to a stop on the roadway. The rider seemed to be studying the house.

Was she a threat? He still saw no signs of any weapon.

Baker kept the motorcycle in sight by glancing over his left shoulder several times as he made his way to the front door.

Ms. Anonymous on the Honda turned in and stopped behind his Trackhawk.

His Trackhawk—she couldn't have it. He felt for the key fob in his pocket and pushed the lock button again for good measure. She couldn't have his M4 either. It was locked up safe inside his SUV.

Baker rapped on the door then let himself in and walked through the entryway to the great room.

Craig and Susan O'Connell sat on the big couch. Zach and Kate Alexander sat beside the couch in a couple of folding chairs, while Steve and Julia occupied the two easy chairs.

Shauna entered from the kitchen and smiled warmly when she looked his way.

He needed to tell Craig about the biker, but one look at Munchkin had nearly erased everything else from his memory.

He walked her way, hooked her arm, and pulled her around until they faced Craig. "Sir, we've got a visitor outside. Followed me on a racing bike from near Terrebonne."

"Someone on a motorcycle?" Craig stood. "Was he armed?"

"I don't think it's a he."

The first four notes of the Westminster chime sounded from Julia's doorbell.

"I've got this." Julia headed toward the door.

"Let me answer, Julia." Craig strode past her.

Steve pulled out his handgun. "Got you covered, sir."

Craig stopped in front of the door and looked out the peephole. "It's a young lady. No weapons that I can see. Just a helmet in her hand. I think were safe." He opened the door. "May I help you?"

"This must be the right house. I followed Mr. Baker here and ... you're Colonel Craig, right?"

"I'm Colonel Craig, but I'm not sure what house you're looking for."

"I'm Airman Gore—at least I was until yesterday. Now I'm just plain old Kathy Gore."

Baker studied her and listened to the exchange from where he stood arm-in-arm with Shauna.

She was slender, as he had thought, about five-foot-eight, bare minimum size to handle a Fireblade.

"Come in, Ms. Gore." Craig motioned toward the great room. "So you're the airman at the Western Air Defense Sector who warned us about the attack."

She nodded.

"There are some grateful people here who would like to thank you for what you did."

"What's she doing here?" Shauna whispered to Baker.

"Let's go find out." He pulled her with him.

Kathy Gore studied them as they approached. "Radley Baker, the pilot. So we finally meet."

"Just call me Beholden Baker, Ms. Gore. You bought me just enough time to outmaneuver the Growler's missile that was chasing my bird's exhaust."

Shauna pulled him snugly against her side. "And I'm beholden Shauna Jackson. Glad to meet you, Kathy Gore."

"Also known as Munchkin," Baker said.

"That's enough, Runt." Shauna dropped his arm and poked his shoulder.

Craig motioned toward the unoccupied end of the couch, beyond Susan. "Why don't you have a seat and tell us what you are doing down here at Crooked River Ranch? Are you on leave, Kathy?"

"More like permanent leave. I wouldn't confess to any violations of the UCMJ, and my commander found out I was in touch with Court & Carpenter, a top-rated, military only law firm. He was afraid to court-martial me, so he got frustrated and agreed to give me an honorable discharge just to get rid of me."

Baker chuckled. "He violated his oath and the Constitution when he ordered the attack on us. He probably realized that an extensive investigation of the incident with that Growler would be much less likely and less productive if you were gone."

"Probably," Kathy said. "But the military's loyalty is divided, so one can't be sure who might be watching you or thinking about prosecuting you."

Shauna dropped Baker's hand and took a step toward the young woman. "On a more pleasant note—can I give you a hug, Kathy Gore?"

"Are you and Baker uh ..."

Shauna gave her a warm hug. "That runt means a lot to everyone here."

"I see," Kathy said, her gaze shifting back and forth between Shauna and Baker.

"So what are you planning to do now that the Air Force discharged you?" Craig said.

"I came here to see if there's anything I can do to help you defend Oregon from President Walker."

Craig gave her his winning smile which slowly morphed to a wry grin. "What do you think you bring to the table, Ms. Gore?"

"Just call me Kathy." She paused. "I still have friends at WADS Headquarters, people who will keep an eye out for you, much like I did."

"I'll bet you have some inside info that would be useful for our intelligence analyst." He glanced at Susan.

Susan walked over and curled an arm around Craig's waist.

If Baker had ever seen one, those two were a matched pair.

Craig reciprocated the arm-around-waist maneuver. "This is Susan O'Connell, part-time barista extraordinaire and full-time intelligence analyst."

Kathy studied Craig and Susan. "Hello, Susan. You know, this seems to be a very friendly place. You are all so ... so ..."

"Coupled up?" Shauna grinned. "We're all either engaged or married."

Baker's head swiveled toward Shauna. "Munchkin, I never popped the question to you. What made you—"

"Yes, you have, Radley Baker. Your memory must be as short as you are. Remember that drive home from Clear Lake?"

"Oh, that." Baker's gaze dropped to the floor.

"Yeah, that."

Kathy's gaze swept the room. "Am I going to fit in with this group? And what about a place to stay out here in the desert?"

"If you agree that Walker is violating the Constitution and must be stopped, you'll fit right in," Craig said.

"About that place to stay—I'm Julia and this is my husband, Steve. We own this house and one of our guests, Zach Tanner, just bought a motorhome and parked it down at the RV park on the ranch. His bedroom is available if you plan to stay."

"I can pay—"

"No, you can't," Julia said. "If you stay, you'll have to share a bathroom with Kate and Shauna. But if you help the militia, you'll more than earn your keep."

After they finished introductions, an electronic device started playing that wild blue yonder song.

Baker quickly focused on the source, Kathy.

She pulled her cell phone from her riding pants pocket. "Excuse me. This could be important." She walked out to the entryway and appeared to have an intense discussion with someone.

"When I heard she was arrested, I thought we had lost a critical source of information," Craig said.

"You mean we lost our guardian angel," Shauna said. "With that pixie cut and her auburn hair, she's pretty cute. Bet she's not a day over twenty. Too bad we don't have any guys in their early—"

"You've gotta let that girl have some time to adjust, Munchkin," Baker said. "She's been through a lot in the past week or two. A boyfriend is probably the last thing on her mind right now."

"You are showing your ignorance of women, Radley Baker."

"Well, I know you. Isn't that knowing a woman?"

"You know choppers and all those gauges and things on the control panel. But knowing a woman is like knowing two dozen different control panels on two dozen airplanes, and—"

"So women are too complicated to know?"

"Radley Baker, right now you don't know—"

"Right now, I only want to know where the throttle is on the control panel to shut that baby down."

Shauna's hands went to her hips. "What **baby**?"

"Your motor mouth, Munchkin."

Kathy's re-entrance into the great room put his war of words with Shauna in a temporary ceasefire but did not terminate the laser sharp looks from her intense brown eyes.

Kathy's visage had changed from the cheerful young woman who had previously left the room. The healthy tan color had drained from her face. She chewed on her lower lip.

The room grew silent.

Kathy sighed as if she was trying to relax. "That was the burner phone I bought to keep in touch with a friend back at WADS. She called because there has been some tell-tale activity at JBLM (Joint Base Lewis McCord), and there are some rumors running around about a big mission. Everyone here may soon be in danger. We think a large-scale attack is imminent involving troops and aircraft from JBLM."

"Why do you think it's a large-scale attack?" Craig asked.

"What would you call fifteen Apaches, four companies of Army Rangers, and enough C-17s to deploy them?"

"A large-scale attack," Craig said.

Steve whistled through his teeth.

"Not good." Craig shook his head. "Any idea when this attack might occur?"

Kathy nodded. "In about four days—maybe a little sooner."

"Everybody, listen up!" Craig scanned the people in the room. "Spread the word to our leaders. We're meeting here at 7:00 p.m.—in three and a half hours. Tell them we're at DEFCON 2 and we're anticipating the largest battle yet in this war with President Walker."

He turned toward Kathy. "Are you sure you want in on this war, Ms. Gore? It's not going to be as safe as working in the Western Air Defense Sector."

"Here I can actually defend the Constitution. I can't think of any other place I'd rather be."

Craig shook her hand. "Then welcome aboard."

Baker looked down into Shauna's dark eyes.

She met his gaze. "I can't think of another place I'd rather be either."

"So I'm forgiven?"

"Baker, I wouldn't count on it if I were you."

Chapter 2

7:00 p.m., Steve's and Julia's house

Shauna had hung out with Baker all afternoon, but he had been unusually quiet. Evidently, the news about an imminent attack and Craig's DEFCON 2 response had occupied his thoughts. That was understandable, but she missed their lively conversation and clever, cutting remarks laced with flirtatious banter.

But as their chief pilot, whatever plans Craig was making to protect their families and the local population would undoubtedly put Radley Baker in the center of the action and the danger.

God had protected them so far in this regional war, but the war was about to escalate in scale and intensity.

Please keep him safe. Keep all our people safe.

"Shall we?" Baker placed two folding chairs across the coffee table from the big couch, completing a big circle that could seat sixteen people in the great room. When the meetings required, they would bring in more folding chairs from Julia's garage.

Shauna nodded and took the seat he offered.

Baker sat beside her and took her hand. His brief glance into her eyes revealed a dark, brooding intensity in his, a look she seldom saw there.

This man had often laughed and joked in the face of extreme danger. But Shauna had only known Baker for a month. Maybe he had a tender heart underneath his muscle and nerves of steel, a deep concern for those he fought to protect.

Craig walked in and took his usual seat in one of the easy chairs at the end of the coffee table.

Susan, his recently proclaimed fiancé, sat in a chair beside him.

These two were a winning combination of wisdom, heart, and when needed, they had a fierceness that should make any potential foe think twice before engaging them in battle. But POTUS wasn't a foe who backed down from any fight even though his military seemed to be fragmenting along with the states and other geopolitical areas.

"Folks, we've got a lot of important issues to cover, so let's get started." Craig turned toward Julia. "Julia, would you open our meeting in prayer?"

Julia nodded and launched into a passionate plea for wisdom, protection, and an outcome pleasing to God that would serve to unite their divided nation.

After his loud amen, Craig glanced at a note card in his hands. "Since defending our troops, families, and others on Crooked River Ranch from attack is our top priority, I contacted Governor Harper to have her put a company of the Guard on high alert to help defend us. And since we now have more Chinooks than we have pilots, I'm requesting some Chinook pilots from Pendleton in case we need to move troops or civilians using our recently confiscated Chinooks."

Steve turned toward Craig. "Colonel Craig, what do we do if Walker is able to amass a large force, one that can simply overrun us?"

"We use CAS, close air support, from the Oregon Air Guard at Kingsley and, if needed, Portland. Each of their F-15 Eagles has a Vulcan rotary cannon, and they can carry up to fifteen 2,000-pound smart bombs, JDAMs."

Craig paused and studied the faces around the circle. "The air guard trains out of Kingsley AFB, so they have a good stock of JDAMs, but we need to use them sparingly, because resupply may not be possible for a while."

Steve chuckled. "Sparingly is a relative term. The lethal radius of a 2,000-pound bomb is larger than a football field, and enemy troops would be wounded, knocked out of the battle, for twice that distance. A single pass over the battlefield by one F-15 could end the battle, unless Walker has a huge army."

"Yep," Baker said. "And our big edge is that Walker has no fighter-interceptors in the entire Northwest. They're all on our side since the air guard took over the Western Air Defense Sector."

"But he does have Apaches from JBLM," Steve said. "However, our F-15s can take them out before they ever reach us."

Craig nodded. "But we need to know where the Apaches are before they get within a hundred miles of the ranch, or we could be in trouble. Likewise for any Chinooks loaded with troops."

Kathy Gore stood. "Colonel Craig?"

"Yes, Kathy."

"Sir, you should know about aircraft headed our way before any of those aircraft get within two hundred miles of here. I'll tell my friends at WADS Headquarters to keep their eyes open and notify us of any possible threats."

"Thanks, Kathy," Craig said. "I'm thankful you chose to throw in with this outfit. We'll do our best to make sure you don't regret it. I'll give you my combat cell number later. Before we move out, be sure to get Susan's cell number so you can give her any intel you get from your friends. She's my analyst."

Susan smirked. "Don't you mean therapist."

"That's only *after* the battle, Susan."

Craig's comeback turned Susan's face red.

Shauna covered her mouth to stifle her laugh.

The rest of the meeting was a planning session for emergency evacuation of the families using vehicles or Chinooks.

As the planning session ended, Kate stood, and the room grew quiet as she scanned each face. "We're going to win this battle and defeat President Walker soundly. But we don't win the war unless we can bring it to a close by unifying the nation."

Craig sighed loudly. "I'm open for ideas on that subject."

"We've exposed the president for what he is and what he's done," Zach said. "Now the opinion of most of the people is swinging against Walker and in favor of the Constitutionalists that want him removed from office."

"But who will replace him?" Craig said. "The VP, Abby Hoffman, is a liberal, but she isn't a radical and probably would not support Walker's unconstitutional actions. I think she's ignorant of the president's black operations that murdered men and made an attempt on a governor's life. What do you think, Lex?"

Lex James, the journalist, sat up in his chair. "Well, we've exposed the president as a murderer. And I believe we could live with the vice president, Abby Hoffman, until the next election. She has distanced herself from Walker's unconstitutional actions. But how do we legally remove a sitting president when Congress can't or won't meet, and while the president is controlling a third of the nation using martial law?"

They needed unity, E Pluribus Unum, one nation under God.

Shauna stood. "However we do this, it needs to end with America completely restored. And we can't afford to create more enemies in the process." She sat again.

Craig swiveled in his chair to face Shauna. "So do you have something in mind?"

That Craig would place any value on her thoughts warmed Shauna's heart toward this leader of men who had allied himself with them. But what if she was wrong and gave them bad advice? But if the advice came from God's word, it couldn't be wrong, could it?

"Well, Shauna?" Craig's eyes weren't harsh or judging, and Craig seldom acted judgmentally.

Okay, Lord. Here goes.

"Zach, Kate and I listened to your program that last week before we all left for Eastern Oregon. You said, 'In each awakening in U.S. history, personal revival led to political change within the culture, because God was changing hearts. That led to a change in votes and that changed who got elected to state legislatures and to Congress.' And you pled with us to pray for a movement of God across our nation. You said that maybe if enough pulpits echoed the call to revival, God would move like He has in the past so that the hearts and minds of millions would be changed, and we would find unity in America once again." She paused. "Then you said that only an act of God could save this nation ... don't you remember, Zach?"

Zach sighed and nodded.

Shauna stood. "Then don't you think you should start calling for every pulpit in this land to echo your words and call this nation to revival?" Her voice crescendoed on the last sentence.

Brock rose and walked to Shauna's side. "She's right, Zach. You're the man with the familiar voice that America listens too."

Zach looked up at Brock. "But you reach millions with your blog."

"It's not the same. They hear your voice, Zach. It has moved people. God willing, it will move a nation. Look, we can fight our battles with President Walker. If God protects us, and we don't do anything stupid, we'll win. Actually, we're pretty good at protecting ourselves. We have some of the finest warfighters on the planet right here in Central Oregon. But that won't restore our nation. It won't grab the warped mind of a radical left proponent and turn it back to God. We can't make this one nation under God until the majority of Americans are willing to submit to God's authority."

"Brock's right," Shauna said. "We're talking some major repentance for some major sins—sins like the abortion of millions of babies, and people personally dishonoring the way God made us as men and women, and the sin of living in immorality of the worst sort. We use some pretty foul language. We even do it in public and think nothing of it. But we aren't just people of unclean lips. Americans are soaked in uncleanness. It's in our minds, our hearts, and it's smeared all over our bodies and tattooed on us. It's in the clothes we wear or the clothes we don't wear. It's everywhere in our culture—TV, movies, the education system, government, in the arts and literature. We're a filthy people. We need to be washed clean by the blood of Jesus, and that starts with the Spirit of God shaking people so hard that they come to their senses and can't stand one more second of what they see in the mirror."

She paused. "Are you listening, Zach? Somebody's got to wake us up. Not like a woke radical, but like it was in the Great Awakening when George Whitefield preached and white folks, Africans, and even Native Americans repented. People from all the colonies shared this. It broke down barriers and united young America. England talked of revolution. France tried it. But nothing like this happened in England or France. Freedom and unity came **only** in America."

Kate put a hand on Shauna's shoulder. "Amen! Keep on preachin', sister. Zach needs to hear this."

Shauna kept her focus on Zach. "Zach, if you're hearing someone, it's not Shauna Jackson. It's God talking to you. So what are you gonna do? Don't tell me you've got some other plan for unity because that isn't possible. We've got nothing in common with those radicals who are so far out in left field that they're in foul territory. But what's not possible with man—"

"Is possible with God." Zach stood. His voice was barely audible, but it stopped Shauna when she saw he was responding.

He blew out a long sigh and his resistance appeared to drain away as he emptied his lungs. "I—I—"

"Come on, Zach. You don't have a speech defect, so don't stutter when you're answering God." Shauna paused and waited.

"I guess God can use me if He wants to."

"Oh, my goodness! That was a powerful statement. Powerfully wussy! I don't want some wimp marrying my best friend. Kate needs a strong man, strong in the Lord. But you're saying, 'Who am I? What am I gonna say? What if people won't listen to me?'

"Zach, you sound just like Moses. Stop giving excuses and start giving yourself permission to call this nation to repentance and unity. Don't make God find somebody else when you have the platform, the ability, and a relationship with the Almighty. He chose us, his people, to do his kingdom work here on this planet. And He chose you to light the fire of an awakening starting right here and right now."

Kate placed her hands on Zach's shoulders and forced him to look into her eyes. "I've known Shauna for over four years. Whenever she gets like this, it's her sensitivity to God's leading. And she's never been wrong yet. But then why would she be wrong? She's just listening to God. Zach, are you listening to her?"

"Yeah. I'm listening." Zach curled his arms around Kate and pulled her into a warm embrace. "Guess it's time to start calling this nation back to God and charging every preacher in every pulpit to do the same."

Shauna clapped her hands. "Hallelujah! We've got a man and a plan to unite these divided states."

Kathy moved alongside Baker. "Is it always this intense when this group gets together?"

Baker chuckled. "Intense? You haven't seen anything yet. Wait until we engage Walker's troops. And like you told us, that engagement may be only hours away."

Chapter 3

9:00 a.m., the next day, Peter Skene Ogden Park, Terrebonne, Oregon

Major Nicholas Deke opened the driver's door of his van and walked across a grassy park and through a stand of cottonwood trees toward what appeared to be a five-hundred-foot-deep gorge. He stopped when he came upon a warning sign.

Caution 300 Ft. Cliff
Warning Hazardous Cliff
Many Dogs Have Died Here
Put your dog back in the vehicle

The picture on the sign showed a dog sailing over the cliff edge.

The picture reminded him of another dog who should be sailing over that cliff, the witch, Julia Weiss—now Julia Bancroft. But he had another place in mind for her death.

Deke peered over the cliff's edge.

A green-blue ribbon wound through a desert canyon that had been cut deeply into the high desert plateau of Central Oregon. A miniature Grand Canyon.

Henderson and Babak approached Deke, slowing as they came close enough to see the depth of the canyon.

Deke turned toward them. "Walker promised to fund us as long as we were making progress. It's time to ask for some funding."

Babak raised an eyebrow. "What progress are you talking about, Deke? Finding a place where dumb dogs die?"

He ignored the obnoxious remark. Babak was always obnoxious. "No. I've got a plan. The militia is always good at anticipating attacks and defending against them."

"That's not much of a plan," Henderson said. "There's nothing to take advantage of."

"We let Walker attack first. We know he's not going to wait much longer. We watch the militia's defensive posture and then attack their weakest spot to go for their weakest members, the women and kids. They'll try to hide them from Walker's troops. We just watch where they go."

"Didn't you try that last time," Babak said. "It didn't go very well, Deke."

"Last time, we didn't know who we would run into when we first encountered them. Had we known, there would have been no surprises and it would have turned out differently."

Henderson smirked. "Are you sure this isn't just a blood raid for revenge? If you aren't careful, this cute dudette is going to get you killed."

"If we get the leaders wives and kids, we have the militia leaders right where we want them ... at our mercy."

***

President Walker took his seat behind his small desk in the private study. He motioned Will Richards, his Secretary of Defense, to take the seat on the other side of the desk.

Will stopped beside the chair and studied Walker for a moment. "Mr. President, are you still trying to make an example of Oregon?"

"Of course. We can't let the first state that defies the federal government be successful. But maybe we've been attacking the wrong side of the state. Maybe we need to eliminate Sandra Harper first. At a minimum, that will throw the Oregon legislature into a state of chaos. Then we can declare martial law and take over."

"So you're going to kill the governor. What will that say to the other governors who support you now? If they displease you, are you coming after them too?" Will paused. "If they feel threatened, they may form an alliance and come after you, Mr. President?"

"What can they do against the massive army I send to annihilate them?"

"You don't have a massive army unless a massive number of troops can be assembled, troops which you can vet and approve, so that you are certain they will obey your commands. If you threaten a warfighter's home state, you're threatening their family and friends. Do that and your own army may turn on you." Will paused. "What happened in Egypt when Morsi tried to rule by force? He couldn't control the military and they took him out. What happened to Hannan nine years ago when he antagonized Army Rangers and Navy SEALs? They came after him, didn't they? And if even one detachment of these Special Forces types decides they are committed to taking you out, you are dead, Mr. President. That is a certainty."

A scene streamed through Walker's mind and he jumped when his phone rang.

Imagining men in tac gear moving through the halls of the West Wing was a ridiculous a response to a few words from a cabinet member. A detachment of Rangers or a SEAL team could not pose a real threat to the most powerful man in the world.

The display indicated Major Deke had called. Walker picked up the phone.

"President Walker. What do you want, Deke?"

"Sir, we have a plan to strike a deadly blow to the Central Oregon Militia, a blow that will take them out of the Oregon equation."

"Why do I have doubts about this? That was supposed to happen last time, but you barely escaped with your life."

"We know how to capture the families of all the militia leaders. This will work like a ransomware attack. These men are mostly Christians. They won't sacrifice their families. They'll surrender."

"And how much will this surrender cost me?"

"I assume you want assurances, Mr. President. We can give you that for two million dollars."

Deke only had a couple of men working with him. How could they use two million dollars' worth of anything?

"Mr. President, this is a deadly blow to the militia. They won't bother you anymore."

"Can you give me that guarantee for one million?"

"No, sir. We need some electronics to hide us and sophisticated weaponry to use in case of an attack. Then a new vehicle, maybe more than one, to transport the prisoners and—"

"Enough! You can have your two million if you promise not to interfere with any of my plans."

"You've got it, Mr. President. Capturing some women and children should not disrupt anything you have planned."

"Okay. Go strike your deadly blow, while I take care of Sandra Harper. But, Deke, the funding is all you get. You're on your own, you have to defend your team, and you'd better stay out of my way. If you interfere with my plans, you're the one who will receive a deadly blow."

Chapter 4

5:00 p.m., Crooked River Ranch, Bancrofts' House

Shauna scanned the doubt-ridden faces of the group sitting in the great room. "I said you have nothing to fear if Craig says we need to evacuate using the Chinook helicopters that we took from the federal troops."

"You're right," Kathy said. I've flown in Chinooks several times. They're safe ... as long as you're not being shot at."

"I meant that I can configure them for any load we need," Shauna said. "Radley showed me how to operate everything inside the cargo bay."

Kate grinned. "So it's **Radley** now?"

Steve and Julia gave each other a knowing nod.

Itzy giggled.

"Okay." Shauna blew out a blast of air. "**Radley the runt** showed me how to load a Chinook. Is that better?"

Baker stood beside her shaking his head. "Munchkin, you can call me whatever you want as long as it's your words. Don't let these verbally challenged people put their words in your mouth."

"That's just it. I didn't, Runt."

Kate stood. "Speaking of words ... Zach should be coming on the air right now over the local station and streamed over his nationwide network. It's his first message since Shauna's little motivational speech."

"Motivational speech? Don't you mean kick in the posterior?" Steve said. "Regardless, we all need to hear what he has to say."

When Julia tuned in the station, Zach had already begun speaking.

"American society is filled with illusions of stability and health. But we are not okay. We are not well. Events occurring on a daily basis prove that beyond any shadow of doubt. What we need is a modern-day Great Awakening to restore the soul of America and provide the glue that has bonded us together in the past.

"However, when a nation models the maliciousness of Molech, sixty-two million times to sixty-two million unborn babies, it must pay for its immorality. The radical left's rapaciousness and anger are only the down payment. God will be the final judge of this nation.

"And now we are sitting on the precipice. As Reagan said fifty years ago, this is the time for choosing. Our choices ... America can either repent or destroy itself.

"This time the enemy lives among us, even in our White House, and wants to enslave us to a Marxist state. We can repent and reject what the enemy offers or remain silent and suffer the destruction of all that we value as Americans.

"How do we reject the Marxism Walker is trying to force on us? We can form a confederacy, maybe I should say a compact of states that wish to remain free. That is, we build a nation within our nation, not entirely separate or we would collapse the infrastructure that supports all Americans and then would fall prey to China and Russia.

"How do we form this compact? We must affirm that all states or regions in the compact adhere strictly to the Constitution, and its amendments, and they must ignore, rebut, and fight with military force, if necessary, to preserve the rights guaranteed to us by the Constitution. A governor of a *free* state should be appointed as the administrator and should invite likeminded states to join the compact.

"The United States of America is a federation of independent states. It's time we acted as such and prevented an overreaching executive from enslaving us to a tyrannical government.

"Remember, folks, Karl Marx, President Walker's idol, was all about destruction. He destroyed his marriage, his kids, and his own body. His destructive forces were his philosophy of life, his economics, and his revolution.

"Take a good look at him, at his depraved life, at the Marxist countries of the world, and learn. Neo-Marxists, and others who subscribe to the cult of the state, take note ... destruction is all that Karl's failed ideology, the cult of the state, ever produced. It kills, steals, and destroys. Sound familiar? If you need a reminder, read John ten, ten in your Bible. Let Jesus himself remind you.

"Just over four decades ago, Ronald Reagan said that everywhere he looked, the cult of the state was dying, dying with the old Soviet Union. While that was true then, and Americans and others benefitted from it, it is no longer true. Today, the cult of the state isn't dying, it's lying. It's the same old lie that the serpent used in the garden, 'You can be like God'. So here we are trying to build another Tower of Babel using Marxist ideology.

"If we are to avoid being deceived, we need to understand where *we* came from and where our successes as a nation came from.

"My fellow Americans, tonight you're going to hear Zach's historical facts. Why? Well, 300 years ago, the American colonies found themselves in a predicament similar to America today.

"In the years between the founding of the colonies and 1726, the first-generation colonists passed on, and control now lay in the hands of second- and third-generation colonists.

"The religious fervor and desire to live a moral life pleasing to God and to work diligently to make a living had been replaced with greed, immorality of every sort, and the churches were languishing in apathy. The love of God had grown cold.

'Now, this didn't happen just among the Puritans in New England, but it was the trend throughout the British colonies.

"No way were these colonies ready for self-government. But in 1726, a time when the secular rationalism of the Enlightenment was darkening Colonial America, a man with a heart for the people began traveling the colonies preaching repentance from sin and salvation through Jesus Christ. George Whitefield preached to everyone he could reach, the common people, American Indians, and the African slaves.

'Even Benjamin Franklin, a man some historians call a deist, was won over by the preaching of Whitefield. Franklin used his printing business to print flyers for all of Whitefield's preaching campaigns. During this time, Franklin was being prepared for his role in preparing our Declaration of Independence, anchoring a constitutional convention, and for bringing the delegates' focus back to God by starting each convention session with prayer.

"The inclusion of the slaves into Christianity paved the way for the abolitionist movement by creating anti-slavery sentiment and moral outrage that eventually became the demise of slavery in America, though it took a war to secure that demise.

"Back to the time period from 1726 to 1776. The Great Awakening emphasized the commonality of colonists as creatures of God, all made in his image. This fostered a unity between the colonies, a unity strong enough to fight and win a war against the strongest army in the world, the British army. This unity prepared the colonies to unite as one nation under God.

"But today, are we one nation? Not really. We're fragmenting under a tyrant, Wendell Walker, the man who does not believe in the very God who unified us through faith in Him.

"We must remember it's not the Constitution that unifies us, because it has been trampled on by two of the last four presidents. It's not even the free-market economy that unites us. Only God unites us through our faith and commitment to Jesus Christ his son. Only He can bridge political parties, racial issues, social classes, age, and gender divides. That's why we need to focus on Him, asking God for spiritual awakening, or we will lose this nation to Satan.

"Once we've united in our shared love of Jesus and acknowledged who our real enemy is, Satan and his minions, then we can have our country back and can discuss the policies needed to prevent the United States of America from ever again becoming the divided states of America.

"So who will join me to pray for the needed revival, to preach to people about it, to provide them reasons for the hope we have in Jesus, and as a result the hope we have for America?

"I want to hear from you. America needs to hear from you. Starting with our next broadcast, we will have an open line that you can call to share your thoughts live on the air.

"Until then, may God bless you, and may God restore and bless the United States of America."

Chapter 5

The next morning, Washington DC, Oval Office

President Walker paced back and forth in front of the Resolute Desk. It was a path he had trod often over the past several weeks, one that might cause wear to show on the presidential seal woven into the carpet.

He stopped when the hallway door near the Roosevelt Room opened, revealing Will Richards.

"Come in, Will. You look like you've been sucking on a dill pickle all morning. What's up, or dare I ask?"

"I'm afraid I've got a dill pickle for you, Mr. President."

"No thanks. I only eat bread and butter pickles."

"I take it you haven't heard about the Oregon Militia's mouthpiece, Zach Tanner, and what he broadcast nationwide last night."

"What kind of sedition is Mr. Tanner preaching now?"

"The kind that gets preached from every pulpit in this country. Mr. President, he's trying to rally all Americans against you. He said you are trying to build a Marxist version of the Tower of Babel. He's trying to get all red states to form a compact of states, under a common agreement, to act together to subvert your authority."

"What did I tell you, Will? It's sedition."

"What are you planning to do about it?"

Walker used his fist as a gavel on the Resolute Desk. "Take down Oregon so it cannot lead this treasonous treachery." He paused. "We need a small, skilled team to sneak in and, no holds barred, capture Harper, and take her from Salem.

"Why?" Will said.

"Because it's the first step in stopping Oregon from leading a rebellion. Harper has Deke's men that were captured in the previous attack. They're still in prison at Salem awaiting trials. Killing her outright would probably keep them imprisoned. And it would bring an all-out attack from the militia."

"Then why don't you hold Governor Harper for ransom. The ransom payment will be freeing Deke's hand-picked team that was captured in that battle by Clear Lake."

"That's not a bad idea, Will. We can also use her to manipulate, or hold off, Craig's militia. Now that she's on their side, the militia won't want to get Harper killed. Regardless that's what must happen once we've accomplished our mission. Since Harper had Layla Thomas arrested, the state treasurer, Ms. Alder, would succeed Harper. But I'm sure, with Harper out of the way, Alder will pardon Layla Thomas who will then become governor by Oregon's rules of succession."

"That's a lot of ifs, Mr. President. And don't forget, you'll have the Oregon Guard on your case and the militia too."

"But I'll have the law and the Constitution on my side. I'll bring the U.S. Army and they will have to obey my commands ... well, if they're still obeying that 'support the constitution' part of their oath."

"Mr. President, it's **defend** the constitution. They might see **defending** it differently than your idea of **supporting** it. What I'm saying is you may have the letter of the law and the Constitution on your side, but not the spirit of it."

"So who's going to stop me, Will?"

"You may be stopping yourself, sir."

"And what's that supposed to mean?"

"That you're wrong, Mr. President."

"I wouldn't push my luck if I were you." He paused and laser focused on Will's eyes. "But if you're determined to take this approach, issue the orders to the black ops commander that you trust the most."

"Frankly, I don't trust anyone we have left."

"Then get somebody the CIA uses."

Will's eyes narrowed. "Nobody can trust the CIA. They have their own agenda and, quite frankly, if they don't like you or what you're doing, they can take you out, just like they did Kennedy."

Assassination? Not in today's world. "And JFK—that's an unproven theory. But we can make sure they like what I'm doing. Toss them a bone and sic them on Harper. You've got your orders, Will. Carry them out."

"Aren't you forgetting something?"

"What?"

"How are you going to defend what comes next. Craig and his militia and probably most of the Oregon Guard will come after you."

"But that's where you come in, Will. While the special forces nab Harper, you will be deploying a large contingent of U.S. Army troops to a convenient location in Eastern Oregon, ready to take out any armed resistance from the militia or the Guard."

Will shook his head. "I'm not sure we can produce a 'large contingent' anymore. Not many in our military want to point guns at American citizens. In fact, a growing number of our troops seem to be talking about the necessity of pointing guns at you."

"A coup? You've got to be joking. They won't come after their president."

"Aren't you forgetting what happened nine years ago? And that effort was led by none other than Captain David Craig, now Colonel Craig, head of the Oregon militia."

Walker swore. "I want at least 5,000 troops to overrun the Guard and Craig's militia."

"So you want a whole brigade?" Will said. "Do you know how long it would take to deploy them? It's weeks, Mr. President. Not hours or days."

"I thought we developed a ninety-six-hour deployment capability anywhere in the world."

"From JBLM ... maybe. But since we wore out our welcome there, so to speak, I thought we were ruling out JBLM."

"I didn't stipulate that."

"Well, if JBLM is in play, one of their Stryker Brigade Combat Teams can lift off ninety-six hours after being given orders. They could start arriving an hour later, somewhere in Eastern Oregon. Normally, that would be over 4,000 soldiers plus about five hundred support personnel to transport them and sustain operations in the field. But presently, with all the division, I'm guessing you can't even get a thousand troops from a brigade. But we would also need a landing strip, one we can control and use as a staging area."

"Find a field. Identify a brigade—as much of a brigade as you can assemble. Spare no expense, or bribe, if it's needed to make it happen. Promise them anything within reason. Like Lincoln did to the confederacy, I want every red state and every red territory to learn what happens when you rebel against the President of the United States of America."

"I can find a staging location. But, Mr. President, Lincoln never tried to punish ... never mind."

Will turned and left the room.

I've got to keep a closer watch on that man.

Chapter 6

10:00 a.m., Crooked River Ranch, Julia Bancroft's house

Baker ended his call with the Pendleton Aviation Regiment. The conversation with the Guard Unit commander there hadn't gone well.

Pendleton couldn't spare any helicopter pilots for at least a couple of days. If Craig and his militia couldn't get the families hidden away from the potential battlefield in less than twenty-four hours, the women and kids could all be killed. Previous actions and intentions said those deaths would weigh on Walker's conscience about as much as a flea on truck scales.

Baker slid his cell into his shorts pocket and walked back into the great room where the strategy session was already underway. "Craig?"

"What did you find out, Baker?"

"We can't use the Chinooks we confiscated from the feds until Pendleton pilots arrive. They said it will take two or three days to free them up."

Craig blew out a loud sigh. "How many family members do we need to move out of here?"

"We've identified everyone the military might know enough about to target," Steve said. "We have right at one hundred women and children."

"I have the list," Susan said.

"It looks like I'm the only pilot available, and my bird is only configured to hold forty-four men," Baker said. "It wouldn't be safe to cram a hundred women and kids into a CH-47."

Craig sighed long and loud. "So it sounds like we're back to driving a fleet of family vehicles to move them?"

Drew nodded. "Sure looks like it, unless Baker has been using some of those long hours he spends with Shauna to teach her how to fly a Chinook."

Shauna's intense brown eyes took aim at Drew. "Watch your mouth, Mr. West, or your luck is about to go south."

"She means it, Drew," Baker said. "Do you need a little motivational speech to prove it?"

"You mean like she gave Zach about—"

"Do I need to call this room to attention?" Craig had raised his voice. "Shauna Jackson and Radley Baker might make a more interesting discussion topic, but we need a plan to get our women, children, and other endangered non-combatants hidden. Several of you grew up in this area. So if we drive them, as has been suggested, where's a safe place?"

"What about McKenzie Bridge," Susan said. "Cedarwood Lodge has six cabins and sleeps about twenty-five. Right next to it is the Log Cabin Inn. It has about twenty-two cabins and should sleep at least seventy-five more. We would have everyone temporarily housed in an area not much bigger than a football field."

"That's about fifteen miles southwest of Clear Lake, Steve said. "It shouldn't be near the fighting."

"Okay," Craig said. "Can you make the arrangements, Susan? We'll compensate the owners of the inns for the cost."

"I grew up there. I know the owners," Susan said. "They'll be glad to help. They probably don't have any guests at either place with all that's happening in the state and after that battle we fought a couple of weeks ago scared everyone off. We were shooting rockets and blowing up Humvees less than twenty miles up the highway. The inns will be available."

"It's time for me to focus on defending against Walker's attack, so I'm putting Susan in charge of the move to McKenzie. She carries an M4. John Peterson has healed from his gunshot wounds, and his family will be evacuating too. I'll send John and his M4 along as added protection."

"Cross me off the list, Susan," Kate said. "Zach's staying at the Redmond Radio station to continue his broadcasts. I'm going to stay there too."

Craig's eyebrows raised. "Are you sure, Kate."

"We'll be fine at the station, Craig. Jared, the station manager, said he has a cot for Zach if he ever needed to stay there. And there's a couch in the women's room."

"Go back to your homes for the night. Pack up what you need for a week-long stay. Meet in the morning where Susan tells you. Then do not go back to your houses for any reason. Don't tell anyone you are leaving. No loose lips. And we don't want any spying eyes knowing where you are going. Susan will give you all further instructions. They're all yours, Susan. All ninety-nine of them."

Shauna looked up into Baker's eyes.

His gaze was fixed on her face.

She lowered her voice. "Radley, only ninety-eight are Susan's. I'm not going with them."

"Yes, you are."

"Am not."

"Don't do this, Munchkin."

She looked away across the room, ignoring him.

"I hate it when you do this. Why, Shauna?"

"Look, Runt. You're going to be flying a Chinook, one way or another. I can help you load it, unload it, and I know how to use an M4."

"It's not safe. I can't let you do that, Shauna."

"How do you plan to stop me, Radley Baker?"

Chapter 7

The next morning, 5:45 a.m., Julia's house

As Shauna's eyes opened, a rhythmical noise pulled her away from her prolonged argument with Baker, an argument that seemed to have lasted the entire restless night.

From across the room came the marimba ringtone on Kathy's cell.

Shauna rubbed her eyes and Kathy's face came into focus. She had answered a call and now held her cell against her cheek.

Kathy's voice grew intense.

Now fully awake, Shauna needed to listen.

"Blair, are you sure the Apache departures were related to the C-17s that took off? ... But you're not supposed to know that. It's classified information. ... I know everything's changed since President Walker made his powerplay, but they can still send you to Leavenworth for telling me. ... I'll pray for you. Now what about their destination? Could you tell where they were headed? ... South and the C-17s climbed slowly like they had a big load? That's concerning. Do you have a vector? ... 155 degrees, straight as a string. What does that intersect near our area in Oregon? ... Prineville. Thanks, Blair. I need to call our commander now. ... Yes, of course we have a commander— he holds the Congressional Medal of Honor. ... No, that's the truth. Thanks again. Got to go now."

What had Shauna just heard? Were they actually under attack? Apaches and cargo planes were in the air right now?

"Kathy, what's happening?"

"My friend from WADS Headquarters just told me that Walker has launched an offensive against us. Apparently, he's using the Prineville airport for a staging area and planes are in the air headed our way right now. I've got to call Craig."

This meant Craig would invoke their evacuation plan, immediately.

Shauna sat up on the edge of her bed as Kathy made the call.

Kathy studied Shauna for a moment then touched her cell's screen.

The ringing of Craig's phone became clearly audible through Kathy's cell. Even in the heat of an emergency, Kathy was considerate enough to let Shauna listen to the call.

"Craig here. What's up, Kathy?"

"My contact at WADS just called to tell me several Apaches and C-17s took off from JBLM a short time ago."

"Did this person know where they were headed?"

Kathy blew out loud sigh. "Prineville, we think. The first C-17s could be there in ten or fifteen minutes. The first Apaches could arrive in a half hour or so."

"So they're going to stage the attack from Prineville. They probably won't attack until they're locked and loaded at Prineville—maybe in three or four hours. But the Apaches worry me. I'm going to notify Susan to start the evacuation. Kathy, tell everyone at Julia's house to prepare to evacuate now. Susan's call chain will notify all the others."

***

Thirty long minutes after receiving Kathy Gore's warning call, Craig sat in the living room of his motor home at the ranch RV park with his militia captains.

They must get this defense plan right. Craig could never live with himself if the families of these remarkable warfighters died because of his mistakes.

Steve's leg was bouncing on the floor like kid on a pogo stick. Craig had only seen this nervous habit once before, when Julia's life was in danger.

"Craig," Steve said. "We can stop this before it even starts. Let's call Kingsley and Portland and have the Oregon Air Guard destroy whatever's on the ground at Prineville. We could hit them so fast they wouldn't have time to prepare for an assault."

"The problem is ..." Craig said, "... they've probably already prepared for that scenario. My guess is that they have Stingers ready to shoot down any of our aircraft that come within range."

Steve's index finger stabbed Prineville on the Oregon map spread out on the table in front of them. "But if our F-15s stay outside of the Stinger's three-mile range, we can destroy any incoming aircraft and what they've already got on the ground. Our Mavericks can hit targets from twelve miles away. They'd be at our mercy."

"Their Sentinel radar will pick us up at twenty miles out," Craig said. "They'll know we're out there."

"But they can't stop us at that range."

"But, Steve, the mission of Kingsley and Portland is Air Defense. They probably have a lot of AIMs, air intercept missiles, but not many air-to-ground missiles."

"Then we need to take down their aircraft before they arrive, while they're still in the air. Then they can't build up a strong force on the ground."

"You're probably right, Steve, but we can't get there in time to get any but possibly the last C-17s. It sure seems a shame to shoot down something as useful and reliable as a C-17."

Steve shook his head. "But that C-17 is carrying death, destruction, and the devil in its cargo bay."

"That's a strange way to describe the weapons our country developed for our national defense."

"But Walker is using them for his **own** defense while he ravages the nation trying to turn it into a Marxist madhouse."

Craig chuckled. "That proves the old admonition that the evil resides in the weapon wielder not the weapon. But we should use the F-15 Eagles for what they were designed to do, protect us by protecting our air space. I'll call the commanders of the 142nd Fighter Wing in Portland and the 173rd Fighter Wing in Klamath Falls to alert them to the invasion and ask them to take down incoming invaders while they're in the air, including any Apaches they send our way. And I'll ask them about providing close air support, CAS, when the ground fighting begins."

"I wonder how the air battles will go," Steve said. "The community of Air Force pilots is a pretty small world. Some of these fighter jocks may know the pilots of the C-17s they'll be asked to shoot down."

"I know," Craig said. "That's the problem with civil wars. In 1861, it was sometimes brother against brother. Pilots are like a band of brothers. I hope the F-15 pilots will be able fire on their targets when asked. Otherwise, we could be in serious danger."

Chapter 8

At 10:00 a.m., Baker glanced across Julia's front lawn at his Trackhawk. He needed to get to the militia's rendezvous by 10:30 a.m. where Craig would give them their orders for the battle against the force from JBLM. Only one obstacle stood in his way.

Susan's voice came from her SUV parked in the driveway. "Come on, Julia. Load your people and let's go. We need to be off the ranch in less than fifteen minutes."

"Itzy, Kathy, Shauna." Julia nodded toward her vehicle. "Grab your packs and let's go."

Shauna, with her pack on her back, scurried to Baker's side. "I'm not going."

"Munchkin, I'm a soldier going into battle. I can't be watching out for a civilian and fight a war. Get in Julia's SUV and follow Susan's orders or I'll—I'll..."

"Or you'll what, Radley Baker?"

"I'll tan your hide."

My hide is naturally tan, thank you. But whether you know it or not, you're going to need me today, Runt."

"What I **need** is for you to get into Julia's SUV."

Shauna's lithe but strong arms circled his neck. "Radley, God showed me what I need to do today."

"Shauna, you're not a conniver. Why are you trying to bring God into this? Regardless, it won't work."

"This day is not going to play out like you think. Just let me come along now, and the first time I distract you from your mission, you can—"

"You're distracting me right now."

Her gorgeous face, large brown eyes so full of life, arms clinging to him—thinking about this kind of stuff was what got men killed on the battlefield.

"All right. Take me along now and if Craig tells me to go, I'll go."

"Is that a promise?"

She nodded. "But it will be okay. You'll see."

Dude, you are a fool.

Susan stood beside her open driver's door, eyes locked on Julia. "What's going on here? Is Shauna coming?"

Julia shrugged.

"No, she's not," Baker said. "God told her to take a slingshot and five smooth stones to meet the Stryker Brigade on the road to Prineville."

Susan wasn't smiling. She glared at Baker.

"She's not going, Susan. She's got her reasons."

"Yeah," Susan said. Reasons of which reason does not know. Whatever you've got cooked up, you'd better watch out for her, Baker, or you'll answer to me." Susan slid into her vehicle and closed the door.

Shauna removed her arms from his neck. "Let's go, Runt. Your Trackhawk is blocking the driveway."

What was he going to say to Craig when Shauna climbed out of his Trackhawk?

Something about convening a court martial, dude. You can count on it.

***

From Deke's look at what had transpired over the past two hours, it appeared that the tall, red-haired beauty was head of the evacuees, and she was driving a brown SUV.

Deke tucked his BF-2050 wide-angle field glasses into their case and slipped behind the juniper tree conveniently located on a rise four-hundred yards from the Bancrofts' house.

He pulled out his sat phone and hit Babak's number.

"Babak here."

"Can you see the brown SUV leaving the house?"

"Yes. Why?"

"Take the Jeep and tail it. Leave the van for me. Call me when you see which way they're headed. And Babak, don't let them see you like you—"

"I won't. Will call as soon as I see which way they go when they leave the ranch."

Forty minutes later, Deke's phone rang. The caller ID said it was Babak.

"Deke, the Trackhawk headed for Highway 97, but the two SUVs went the opposite direction to Sisters, then they took Highway 242."

"That's a little farther than just leaving the ranch. Why didn't you call earlier? Forget it. Just call me and let me know which way they go when they reach Highway 126." He ended the call.

It was twelve thirty when Deke drove through Sisters. In a couple of minutes, he turned onto Highway 242. His stomach was grumbling. All he'd had for breakfast was coffee.

A school came into view on his right.

Since school wasn't in session, Deke pulled into the parking lot and backed into a parking space.

He found an MRE in the box of supplies in the cargo area and downed it cold.

If Babak and Henderson hadn't taken any in the Jeep, they would be more than hungry at dinnertime, but they would survive, unlike one Julia Bancroft.

When Deke pulled out of the parking space, his phone rang. It was 1:00 p.m., almost three hours after the brown SUV pulled away from the Bancrofts' house. Maybe Babak had some good news.

"Deke, we know where the civilians plan to hide. It looks like they're using two adjacent resorts near McKenzie."

"Resorts? Are they like lodges or individual cabins."

"Individual cabins. Very individual. Hidden in the trees, but they're all within a one-hundred-yard radius."

"I want to know which cabin Julia Bancroft is staying in. If you can, without revealing your presence, map out a path we can use to breach that cabin during the night. And I want to know who else is staying in that cabin with her."

"Will do, Deke."

Deke ended the call and placed another one.

"Mr. President, Colonel Deke here."

"Deke, Stryker Brigade is on their way to crush the militia. Stay out of their way."

"Sir, crush may be a bit optimistic. First, you can't assemble a whole brigade in this fragmented nation and fragmented military. You've only got five or six hundred troops at most. Second, the militia commander, Colonel Craig, will not let you crush any part of his army."

"You know what? You're just like your brother and will likely end up like him, dead."

Deke squeezed the drink from his MRE until its contents sprayed the headliner of his van. Walker knew how to push Deke's hot buttons and it galled him that he could be manipulated so easily.

He took a breath to control his voice. "Mr. President, I've located the families of the militia leaders. After we take some of the key members, maybe the militia will be ready to negotiate a surrender. That would be a pretty feather in your Make-America-Irate-Again cap."

"Cute, Deke. But we are not preparing to negotiate until they offer to surrender. For now, Stryker Brigade is preparing to attack, and they will crush Craig's militia with our overpowering ground force and a fleet of Apache helicopters."

"I hope you're right, Mr. President. If Stryker Brigade Commander, Colonel Blackford, wants to know where the families are hiding, tell him to call me. Goodbye, Mr. President."

"Deke, you're not the one giving ord—"

Deke ended the call.

The only order I want to give is the one that ends the life of my brother's murderer, Julia Bancroft.

Chapter 9

2:00 p.m., a patch of desert along Terrebonne-Lower Bridge Road

Foremost on David Craig's mind was that a force larger than his militia was preparing to attack. But the devil is always in the details, and Craig believed the adage that one should always "know thine enemy." The problem was, due to the terrain, he could not get enough detailed intelligence from his sentries posted east of Redmond.

The devil was still hidden somewhere near Prineville. The mountains west of Prineville had only one break in them, the Crooked River Gorge. Craig couldn't move his sentries close enough to Prineville to view the activity at the airport where he feared the Stryker Brigade was staging a massive attack.

Craig's main force had assembled in an area of state-owned land along Terrebonne-Lower Bridge Road at the south end of Crooked River Ranch.

"Craig, sir." Steve approached him, but he glanced back several times at the hundreds of men milling around in the three or four acres of desert they occupied. "The men are wondering how long we're going to hold up here in this patch of desert."

"Steve, we need to remain deployed near the ranch to protect our homes, and the other civilians that live among us, if the ranch is attacked first. From here, we also have quick access to roads going east, west, north, or south. We can deploy to other areas once we learn where the troops from JBLM plan to attack."

"What should I tell the men, Craig? They're getting restless. It's two o'clock and the temperature is almost one-hundred degrees out here."

"Tell them I'm contacting Colonel Whittingham, commander of 173rd Fighter Wing at Kingsley. He should have engaged some of the aircraft near Prineville by now, and his F-15 pilots should have a good idea about the size of the force we're up against and how close they are to being combat ready. We'll have some actionable intelligence in a few minutes."

"Thanks, sir. I'll spread the word."

As Steve turned and walked back to the militia troops, Craig pulled out his sat phone and hit the entry in his contacts list for Colonel Whittingham.

"Whittingham here."

"Colonel, this is David Craig, Oregon Militia. Our main force is assembled, but we're waiting to get some intel before making a move. Have your pilots reported on the activity near Prineville yet?"

"We've kept two Eagles in the air near Prineville for the last hour and a half. They arrived as the last C-17 was crossing into Oregon between Pendleton and the Dalles."

"Did your pilots tell them they were violating the air space of the sovereign state of Oregon?"

"They did. The C-17 pilot ignored all warnings, so our Eagle took the intruder down."

"That's too bad. But now JBLM knows they can't enter Oregon air space at will. What did your pilots see on the ground near Prineville?"

"We have one of our Eagles on the radio right now. Do you want me to patch you in?"

"That would be great, Colonel."

The line went dead for a few seconds, then came to life with the crackle of static.

"This is Eagle niner niner two. An Apache enroute to Prineville fired a Stinger at me. I avoided it with countermeasures. This validates our suspicion that those birds are carrying Stinger missiles."

"Command post here, Eagle niner niner two. Have you verified suspected deployments of Stingers on the ground?"

"Eagle niner niner two, Stingers are deployed around the airfield at a radius of about three miles. It looks like they want to protect the airfield out to about six miles, which would prevent us from interfering with their staging activity. Do you want me to take out the deployed Stingers?"

"Command post here. That's a negative, niner niner two. Remain in the area and report on ground troop activity until you need to return for fuel."

"Roger, command post. Ground troops don't appear to be in a hurry. They are taking their time. Eagle niner niner two circling the airfield at a radius of eight miles as long as fuel permits."

The F-15 pilot signed off and the call went back to Craig and the wing commander.

"Colonel Whittingham, if the ground troops aren't in a hurry, it sounds like they may be planning an attack for tonight or maybe daybreak tomorrow."

"I would agree, Craig."

"I've got a question for you, Colonel," Craig said.

"Fire away."

"If it turns out the brigade plans to target Crooked River Ranch to destroy the militia members' homes and possibly kill other civilians on the ranch, can we count on your fighter wing for CAS if needed?"

"You sure can. And you can count on the 142nd Fighter Wing in Portland for CAS also. I will have both wings on high alert. We can be in your area bombing the heck out of the enemy within twenty minutes of receiving your call. Maybe within fifteen minutes."

"That's music to my ears, Colonel Whittingham."

Whittingham chuckled. "It's always good to know you have air superiority, isn't it, Craig?"

"Yes, sir," Craig said. "And the Stryker Brigade isn't used to fighting under those circumstances. This is much different than Afghanistan. Got to go now and brief my troops on what I just learned. Let us know if your pilots report anything significant such as ground troops moving out."

"Will do, Craig."

"One thing we must accomplish Colonel Whittingham— we can't let a single Apache make it as far as Crooked River Ranch. They could wreak havoc there. And we can't let them reach my troops."

"We've got you covered, Craig. Each Eagle can take on several Apaches and prevail."

"Thanks, Whittingham." Craig ended the call and walked toward the large gathering of militia troops.

"Men, listen up. Stryker Brigade apparently is gearing up for an attack on some area in the vicinity of the ranch either late tonight or first thing in the morning. We have assurances of CAS from Kingsley and Portland. They will remain on alert and will be here within a few minutes of a call for help. I also have assurances from the Oregon Air Guard that they will not let any Apaches survive to reach the ranch. Our homes and other civilians there are safe. Kingsley is maintaining air surveillance of the brigade and will alert us if they start to deploy. We'll prepare to move out after we get word from Kingsley."

Craig ended his short briefing with a word of encouragement about their air superiority. But one disquieting thought niggled.

The Stryker Brigade should be in a bigger hurry than they appeared to be. What if the brigade somehow knew where the militia families had been taken? Would that account for what the intel reports were telling him?

Chapter 10

8:30 p.m., Mahonia Hall, governor's mansion, Salem

At least a dozen conversations today discussing how to defend the state in light of an imminent attack had left Sandra Harper mentally and emotionally exhausted. It was a little after 8:30 p.m. when she slid out of her limo at Mahonia Hall, her residence for as long as she could hold onto both the state and the office of governor.

After the limo pulled away, she paused and looked westward.

The sun hovered above the coastal mountains to the northwest, where puffy clouds lingered from the afternoon. The sun would set in a few minutes and it should be a spectacular display of light and color, unlike Sandra's day behind the governor's desk. Kate would have called the brewing sunset God's masterpiece.

Despite the present trouble, Sandra had much to be thankful for—her beautiful niece, Kate, who still loved her despite their big misunderstanding a few weeks ago, the securing of the state by the compact made between her and the militia, and two successful military rebuffs of attacks against Oregon ordered by President Walker. And Sandra had survived two attempts on her life.

When she listed those events end-to-end, the current ending seemed highly improbable, almost like she was being protected. A few weeks ago, she would have deemed that notion absurd. But now ... she wasn't sure.

She hurried inside, greeted the officer at the door, and scurried to her room to change into something more comfortable before she roamed the lush gardens and watched the solar spectacle.

Five minutes later, she was strolling through the impeccably manicured garden.

The sun had perched on a peak in the coastal range and would soon drop below the horizon. That would set the sky on fire.

Footsteps sounded on the walkway behind her.

Maybe it was too much to expect a few minutes of peace in the midst of the present crisis.

She turned and looked down the walkway. Who was the uniformed officer? It looked like Williams, but with the man's hat pulled low, she wasn't sure.

"Officer Williams?"

He stopped about five feet from her. Near his body, partly concealed, he held a gun. He had pointed it directly at her.

"Williams works, but not a peep or warning cry from you or Layla Thomas will be sworn in as governor tonight. Do you understand?"

The surrealism of the moment morphed to reality and she stifled a gasp. She needed to stay calm and think.

"I said, do you understand, Ms. Harper?"

Sandra tried to focus on the man and his words, but she realized her gaze darted from bush to bush in the garden looking for a place—

"You can stop looking around. No one is coming. However, you are going to come with me to the driveway."

He nudged her toward the circle drive, and she began walking slowly.

The gun had disappeared to some concealed place on his body.

"Nice try, whoever you are. But you'll never get me off this property, so why should I go with you to the driveway?" That statement would probably cause trouble for her, but it was the only comeback she could think of as she began the precarious process of stalling.

"Not simply a nice try, Governor. Rather it's a plan perfectly executed. And if you stop cooperating at any point, **you** will be perfectly executed."

Her eyes widened, though she tried to stop her response.

"I see that I've gotten your attention. I suggest that you let me keep it. That might keep you alive."

When she saw the circle drive, a limo sat in it, a limo that looked identical to one she often used.

"Yes, it's a twin, Governor Harper. Not an identical twin. It lacks the armor, bulletproof glass, and communications equipment, but close enough for government work." He laughed softly.

Heat rose at the back of her neck. This thick-headed thug was about to receive the toe of her shoe in a painful place.

"Whatever you're thinking, I suggest that you think again. You are wanted dead or alive, and I'm finding fewer reasons to keep you alive every time I look at your face."

She whirled toward him.

The gun came out of nowhere and jammed into her rib cage.

She winced from the pain.

"Get in the limo, Ms. Harper. Your usual seat."

"What makes you think you can get me through the gate?"

"Didn't I tell you? You have a new gatekeeper. Jim had a fatal accident."

This man and his cohorts had killed part of her security team. But even if they took her off the property, they still had to get out of Salem. And within fifteen minutes, every policeman in the state would be alerted as would the National Guard.

The thugs could kill her if they wanted to, but they would have done that already if that was their plan. That raised a disturbing question. What did they want to do with a living, breathing Sandra Harper? That question led to another more unsettling one. How long would they allow her to keep living and breathing?

This guy had mentioned Layla Thomas, a Walker supporter and the successor to the governorship should anything happen to Sandra. That must be part of the reason they had woven together such an intricate plan to capture her.

But Colonel Craig was anticipating an attack ordered by President Walker and indicated in a phone call today that there were signs the assault had already begun.

Her captors were fools if they thought this could deter Craig and the militia. But it might cause some distraction, maybe causing Craig to split his militia force to fight on two fronts, especially if Layla Thomas was to be sworn in as governor.

The limo left through the Mahonia Hall gate without a hitch. Who was Sandra Harper on the road with? Only one rational answer came to mind. She was the captive of a team of killers with a plan to retake Oregon from those who supported the Constitution.

Regardless of the details of the killers' plan or the goals of the perpetrators, one thing was sure.

They won't let me come back to Salem alive.

Chapter 11

10:30 p.m., Terrebonne-Lower Bridge Road

At 2230 Craig's sat phone rang. The caller ID displayed the command post at Kingsley Air Force Base.

"Colonel Craig here."

"Craig, this is Captain Sorenson, Kingsley Command Post. The colonel said to let you know if we noted any troop movement from Prineville."

"Isn't it dark now at Prineville?"

"Yes, sir. But about thirty minutes ago, as our last sortie turned to come home, he saw troops leaving, going north on Highway 26 toward Madras."

"Thanks, Sorenson. That tells us where they might attack."

"Sir, we'll be in the air again at first light, about 0430."

"A quick question, Sorenson. Did any pilots report seeing Chinooks or Blackhawks on the ground at Prineville?"

"Let me check." The line went silent for about ten seconds. "Yes. At about 1600 we received a report of a possible Blackhawk among the fifteen Apaches."

"Only one?"

"That's what the report indicates."

"Thanks, Sorenson." Craig ended the call.

Steve watched with curiosity as Craig tucked his phone in its pocket.

"Steve, that was Kingsley command post. Here's a question for you. Why would Stryker Brigade not bring in some birds for rapid deployment of the troops? There's only one, a Blackhawk on the ground at Prineville and no Chinooks."

"Maybe because we stopped them from getting here, thanks to Airmen Gore and her friends up north."

"I hope you're right. Well, the troops are moving, and it looks like they're headed toward the ranch, via Madras."

"But that puts them on the wrong side of the Crooked River Gorge."

"Maybe they have cannons and rockets to take out our homes from the butte on the east side of the gorge. Two thirds of our homes would be in easy range from there."

"But, Colonel Craig, that's only a small moral victory for such a large deployment."

"I know. But I haven't been able to come up with a better explanation. But in case we need to move some of our troops more quickly, I had Baker and Shauna prepare one Chinook at Madras with everything we had up there, ammo, Humvees, food, and water, and another for transporting just our troops. Sure wish Pendleton would free up a couple of Chinook pilots to help."

"Didn't they say maybe by tomorrow night?" Steve asked.

"The way this is going, tomorrow night will be twenty-four hours too late."

Steve sighed. "Well, Baker's Trackhawk just drove up. Isn't it supposed to be bad luck to have a woman in a combat camp?"

"In war, you can't afford to depend on luck, good luck or bad luck," Craig said. "Tell the men to get some rest. In a couple of hours, we should know what Stryker brigade has up their sleeve. We can hold them away from the ranch for a while, if we need to, then have the air guard deal them a knockout punch after daybreak."

Steve walked away toward the largest group of men.

Baker and Shauna took Steve's place beside Craig.

"Colonel Craig, we have a Chinook ready to move up to forty-four men with their packs."

Craig nodded. "I'll keep that in mind." He turned toward Shauna. "How's it going?"

"I'm glad I can help, Craig. Everyone needs to pull their weight around here if we're going to defend Oregon."

"Baker put his arm around her waist. "A hundred and ten pounds isn't much weight to pull. And she's a quick study."

Craig studied the arm around Shauna's waist. "Just make sure your studies stick to the curriculum, Baker."

"Wouldn't think of doing anything else, sir."

Even in the dim light in the camp, Craig could see Shauna's eyes roll.

"Get some rest. It looks like we could be moving out in two or three hours."

"Where to, sir," Baker pulled his arm from Shauna's waist.

"That depends upon when intel tells us what Stryker Brigade is up to. But like I said, you need to get some rest. Tomorrow starts early and it's going to be a long day."

Craig put Steve in charge of the guard duty for the militia company and settled into the seat of his SUV to rest.

An annoying ring sounded somewhere in the distance. As the grogginess of sleep wore off, Craig recognized the alarm coming from his sat phone. He pulled it out. 0315. And the display indicated the sentry near Suttle Lake was calling.

"Colonel Craig here."

"Sir, this is Al Lopez at checkpoint five. It looks like the whole Stryker Brigade is moving down Highway 20 headed toward the intersection with Highway 126."

That wasn't possible. Craig had placed a sentry on La Follette Butte, along Lower Bridge-Market Road to watch the area south of the ranch. That would have given warning of an attack from the south. But with a short row of hills in the way, the sentry wouldn't have been able to see activity three miles south along Highway 126, especially if Stryker Brigade ran without lights using their nighttime vision.

"Lopez, how fast are they moving?"

"About twenty-five to thirty miles-per-hour. And they're running without any lights. But we don't have any people out this way, do we?"

"No. We have no militia out there. Thanks, Lopez. I'll decide how to respond. Keep watching them and report if you see anything changing."

"Yes, sir."

Craig punched the icon to end the call.

It wasn't possible that Stryker knew where the militia had hidden their families, was it? And how did four hundred troops get from heading to Madras to headed for McKenzie?

The Forest Service roads? They must have used them to cut through to Highway 97, then hit Highway 126 at Redmond. That would have sent the Stryker Brigade about three miles south of the sentry Craig had placed on La Follette Butte. With hills between them, the sentry would never have spotted them.

Eluding his sentries in this manner couldn't be a coincidence. The Stryker Brigade must have gotten information from someone in the local area.

Was Craig dealing with a traitor or a spy? Regardless, he had to move out now to head off the Stryker Brigade before they got anywhere near the women and kids at McKenzie.

But could this be a trap to lure the militia? It didn't matter. All that mattered was stopping those troops ASAP.

Craig walked to where the men had congregated. "Listen up, men! We've got an emergency. The Stryker Brigade has bypassed our sentries and is moving along Highway 20 not far from the intersection with Highway 126. At the speed they're traveling, we've only got an hour and half to intercept them and slow them down. We need stop them long enough to evacuate the families. We've got about ten minutes max to come up with a plan and then move at full speed on Highway 242 to cut the brigade off on 126. I need a plan to stop the Stryker Brigade and an evacuation plan that works using the people we have right here."

"What about having the women and kids make a run for Klamath Falls right now?" Drew asked.

"I thought about that," Craig said. "But it's a three-and-a-half-hour drive to Kingsley AFB. And there are a couple of other reasons why I believe it's a bad idea. First, we think there is a Walker spy in the area or, heaven forbid, a traitor in the militia informing Walker. Second, if Walker's force decided to send all of the Apaches after our families, I'm not sure if even the entire fighter wing could guarantee their safety, especially if the Apaches all flew different routes to their target. Getting the women and children to Kingsley is the right move, we just need a safe way to accomplish that."

Drew moved close to Craig and spoke slightly above a whisper. "If we let that force from JBLM capture our families, we will lose this war, we'll lose Oregon, and maybe even this broken nation."

Craig sighed long and loud and nodded slowly. "Thanks for the encouragement, Mr. West."

Chapter 12

Baker hooked Shauna's arm and pulled her behind his Trackhawk, out of hearing distance of Craig. "Did you hear Craig? We've only got an hour and a half to evacuate the families."

Shauna nodded. "I've never seen Craig look so worried. We could go back and get a Chinook to fly them out to a safe place."

Baker shook his head. "A Chinook is too slow, and it can't carry all the people. But ..."

"Radley Baker, I don't like the look in your eyes and don't leave me hanging like that. But what?"

"We need one of those C-17s sitting on the tarmac at Prineville."

"I think the runt just lost his mind. A Chinook might be too slow, but at least it can land to pick up people. Besides, how are we going to steal a C-17 on a heavily guarded tarmac at Prineville?"

"Listen for a minute, Shauna. There's a landing strip by McKenzie Bridge. Look it up on your cell. We need to do some math in a hurry."

"So we're just gonna skip the problem of stealing a C-17?" Shauna pulled out her cell and keyed in *landing strip by McKenzie Bridge*. "I'm pretty good at math. What do we need to calculate?"

"Select the airnav website link and give me the details about the airfield."

"It's called the McKenzie Bridge State Airport. The field's 2,600 feet long, but it says there are obstructions at the end of the runway."

"What kind of obstructions? Trees?"

"Yes. There are trees a hundred-and-twenty-five-feet-tall at one end about fourteen hundred feet out from the runway."

"Okay, mathematical Munchkin, what's the climb rate I need to clear those trees?"

"Climb rate?"

"What angle will keep me from hitting those trees?"

"Uh, well, it's gonna be the arctangent of a hundred twenty-five over fourteen hundred."

"Great. Like that's going to help me."

"Just a minute." Shauna thumbed furiously on her cell. "Climb rate's about five point one degrees."

"Have you got a trig calculator app or something?"

"Or something. It's a website called Rapid Tables."

"Okay. Five point one degrees. I don't know what the max climb rate of this bird is."

"It won't be empty, Baker. We could have a hundred people onboard."

"With a full load we'd probably never make it out of there. But a full load for a C-17, if I remember correctly, is three Bradley's, a lot of equipment, and a few dozen men crammed in around the cargo. I don't think a hundred people weigh nearly that much."

"Wait. I've got a video that says it's gonna display the maximum climb rate of a C-17 Globemaster."

"Look, dwarf, a video doesn't cut it. I need the real numbers, the angles."

"Dwarf? What happened to Munchkin, Runt?"

"Munchkin got munched up in a C-17 crash. Didn't you hear?"

"I'll deal with you later, Baker. But right now I've paused the video after the Globemaster lifted off. Wanna see it climbing?"

"No. I want to see the numbers. The climbing angle."

"Okay. Wait a minute. "

He stuck his head over her shoulder. "Good grief! Don't tell me you're gonna use a protractor? This isn't Geometry class. Besides, where are you going to find a protractor in the desert in the middle of the night?"

"Got one right here on my cell—at learner worksheet dot com."

"Shauna, this is not the way you determine if a takeoff over high obstacles is safe. You need tables constructed by flight engineers."

"Got any better ideas, Runt?"

He didn't reply.

Shauna's gaze locked on her cell's display. "Oh, my. Look at this."

Baker leaned closer to see the screen. "Look at what?"

"The C-17 took off at a thirty-five-degree angle, and it just kept on climbing."

Baker blew out a long sigh and laid a hand on her arm.

She looked up at him, studying his face.

He pulled her close and kissed her forehead. "Thanks, Shauna. I was lost without my pilot's manuals. But we can do this. Thirty-five degrees will clear anything around, even if we lose a little of the angle with a hundred people onboard."

"I'll accept your apology if you promise never to call me dwarf again. I'm short, but I'm not that short."

"Then I promise." He squeezed her arm. "You've got a quick mind and a quick tongue."

She rolled her eyes. "Baker, sometimes your tongue is a lot quicker than your mind."

This wasn't the time to search his vocabulary-challenged mind for an equally prickly reply.

"Come on." Baker tugged on Shauna's arm. "We've got to stop Craig. It looks like he's through planning and ready to move out. He needs to know our plan and factor it in."

The two scurried around the Trackhawk and up to Craig's side.

Baker cleared his throat. "Craig, sir?"

"Make it quick, Baker. We're moving out."

"We have a plan to safely evacuate our families if you can hold the brigade well north of McKenzie until 0545."

"First, who's we?"

"Shauna and I."

Craig blew out a blast of air and started to turn away.

"Craig, this **will** work."

Craig faced Baker. "This group would have to hold off the entire brigade for at least an hour. We'd need to do it near Clear Lake to keep them a safe distance from McKenzie."

Shauna stepped beside Baker. "Last time you wiped them out at Clear Lake."

"And last time we had superior fire power."

"But wouldn't you have air superiority?" Baker said.

"Not until it's light enough to use close air support safely. We'd have to hold them at least thirty minutes on our own. Remember, they could decide to sic the Apaches on us, Baker."

"But the F-15s can defend against Apaches even before first light."

"Okay. I've invested two minutes that I can't get back. Let's hear your plan."

"Well, it depends on getting Shauna and me to Prineville by 0500."

"You and Shauna? To Prineville in ninety minutes? And what do you plan to do in Prineville? Get yourselves killed?"

"No, sir. We're going to steal a C-17 and evacuate our women and the kids."

"Have you been smoking that weed they grow on the other side of the Cascades?"

"Colonel Craig, we can do this if you can get us a pilot."

"What the—Baker, you *are* a pilot."

"Sir, there's an old pilot in our group who flies a Cessna out of Redmond, Daggett. He can get me to Prineville."

"Yes, and you can get him killed in the process."

"We're wasting minutes, sir. Just call him and see if he can fly me to Prineville."

Shauna leaned close and whispered to Baker, "Let's pray he can reach Daggett."

Craig glanced up at Shauna. "I can reach him. He's our sentry posted east of Redmond, watching the Prineville area."

Baker watched as Craig hit the speakerphone toggle on his sat phone.

"Bob Daggett here."

"Colonel Craig here. Daggett, are you up for a little adventure?"

"If it involves flying, I'm always up for some adventure."

"Maybe you'd better hear what I'm proposing first."

"Anything beats standing on the hilltop, craning my neck to see what's just over those hills that block my view of the Prineville airport. Shoot, sir."

"How soon can you be ready to take off?"

"You mean in my Cessna?"

"Yes. With a passenger."

Shauna tapped Craig's shoulder and put up two fingers.

Craig mumbled something under his breath. "Make that two passengers."

"I can get back to the airport in ten minutes. Then I've got to check out a few things and fill the tank. I can be ready by 4:30 a.m. Where are we going?"

"To Prineville."

"Sir, I was just about to call you. A short time ago, I saw lights of aircraft off to the east. They were so thick they looked like a bunch of buzzards circling roadkill near Prineville."

"Yeah. That's going to be a problem you'll have to deal with. You won't be welcome there."

"Craig, I can deal with that while we're on our way," Baker said.

"I've got some friends at the airport," Daggett said. "They'll speak up for me with the military. But if we try to land while it's dark, they'll just shoot us down before we get there. We shouldn't try to land until it's light."

"That's about 0430," Craig said.

"Who are my passengers?"

"Our pilot, Baker—"

"Great. This is sounding more fun all the time."

"The other passenger is Shauna Jackson."

The other end went silent.

"You mean that cute little gal Baker's been hanging around with?"

"That's her."

"Well I'll be. Now I've got to keep two people out of trouble at Prineville."

"This is Baker, Daggett. We'll work out all the details while we're in the air. You only have to worry about flying over and landing safely. We'll take care of ourselves."

"You need to leave now, son, if we're gonna make it by four-thirty. Come in on Southeast Salmon Avenue. It's north of the terminal. Meet me in the parking lot for the Hillsboro Aero Academy. You'll see it on your left as you drive in."

"Got it," Baker said and he motioned for Craig to end the call.

"They're leaving right now, Daggett." Craig tapped the screen of his phone.

"If we take off at 0430, we'll get to Prineville at 0500," Baker said. "It'll take fifteen minutes more to steal a C-17. Then it's sixty-five miles at 450 miles-per-hour—that's fifteen minutes to get to McKenzie Bridge State Airport. It will take at least fifteen minutes to load everyone and take off. That's one hour and fifteen minutes from the time we leave Redmond with Daggett. We can be evacuating the families by about 0545. Can you hold the brigade off that long, Craig?"

Craig shook his head. Was he saying no or just not buying into Baker's plan?

"Stryker Brigade could get there as early as 0445. Somehow, we will hold them. For an hour if we have to. But, Baker, I think your plan is crazy. Do you realize how many points of failure there are along the way?"

"It only sounds crazy. That's why it will work. They'll never believe what's happening in Prineville. It's crazy to try to steal a C-17 right out from under their noses. They won't be expecting it. And there's only one point of failure. We either commandeer the plane or they commandeer us. We can do this, Craig. You head off the brigade, slow them down a bit, and I'll fly our families out."

"I was on the verge of ordering you not to go."

"I'm glad you didn't. I've never disobeyed orders before, but I would have had to."

"And I'd have revoked them if you had." Craig smiled. "Be careful, Baker."

"You can count on that, sir. Munchkin will be with me. She understands the risks and ... I couldn't pull this off without her."

"Baker, distractions are deadly when you're on a mission like this. You're already pushing beyond any sane limits."

"Sir, have you forgotten that Susan's with the families?"

"I haven't forgotten anything. And I'd like to forget how many rules of combat strategy I'm violating here."

"Will you call them and tell them I'm coming at about 0530 in a big cargo plane."

"I put Susan in charge of the families. I'll call her now. And I'll tell them to stay three hundred yards from the runway when you try to land a Globemaster on that backwoods airstrip."

"Gee, thanks for the confidence."

"He's got more sense than you, Mr. Baker," Shauna said.

"That doesn't say much for you, Munchkin. You won't have the option of staying three hundred yards from the runway."

"I was sort of hoping to be on the runway and not in—what do they call a crash site?"

"A smoking hole," Baker said.

Chapter 13

4:30 a.m., Roberts Field, Redmond

Baker buckled in his seat on the little Cessna and watched Shauna do the same. She was grace and beauty wrapped up in a—that was not part of the curriculum Craig had mentioned. If Baker couldn't keep his head in the game, he might get it shot off by troops at Prineville.

The geriatric pilot, Bob Daggett, was good for his word. At 0430 he taxied his blue and white Cessna 150 to takeoff position at Roberts Field.

"I have a hangar at the Prineville airport. Used it when I flew sky divers out of Prineville and when I worked on my Cessna. I can fly you and Munchkin to the Prineville airport. If I'm clever enough, I can land without getting us shot up or shot down. I'll make up some kind of emergency. Maybe I can taxi close enough to a C-17 to get you into one. If I can't, we can taxi into my hangar and think of some other way to steal one of those big birds." Daggett paused. "So how many hours have you got on C-17s?"

The truth was going to come out one way or another. Baker sighed. "About 2 hours."

"Shoot, son. You're gonna get yourself and this little lady—"

"In a simulator," Baker added then cringed waiting for the reply.

"Two hours in a simulator? So you're really winging it, so to speak."

"Literally."

"You know that's plumb loco. If the guards don't shoot you on the tarmac, you'll both end up in a smokin' hole in that bird right after takeoff or wherever you try to land it. By the way, where are you landing it?"

Here comes another one. "McKenzie Bridge State Airport."

"Down by the South Sister? Refresh my mind, son. How long is that landing strip?"

Baker blew out another sigh. "The airfield's twenty-six-hundred-feet long."

"What have you got between those ears, son?"

"I'm not your son, Daggett."

"And I'm grateful for that. A man should never have to see his children die before he does." He blew out a blast of air. "Supposin' you get that bird down. How are you gonna get out of there. We did that sorta' thing with short airstrips a few times in Nam with JATO, you know, jet assisted takeoff, but—"

"You let me worry about that. We don't need jet assistance. This bird has a lot more power than those old C-130s you used in Vietnam."

"A Globemaster landing and taking off from that field—plumb crazy."

"We're going to have a hundred people onboard. I don't plan to get them killed."

"Women and kids you say?"

"That's right."

"Well, man makes his plans and the Lord Almighty directs his steps. I'll sure be prayin' He directs yours."

Daggett opened the throttle and the little Cessna accelerated down the runway.

Shauna had given him three or four of those your-crazy looks. Baker needed to end the talk about craziness and smoking holes.

Once they were in the air, he leaned forward and raised his voice above the drone of the engine. "How about we go over what we're doing at Prineville."

"Back to Prineville," Daggett said. "Where my hanger is located and the way the wind is blowing, I'll probably have to taxi right by all of those big birds on the way over. You two bail out on the side opposite the buildings. There's nothing but runway and desert on that side. With a C-17 blocking their view—they sit purty close to the ground—nobody in the airport can see you."

"But we need to find a bird with the front door open," Baker said.

Daggett chuckled. "Don't you mean with the door open and nobody around?"

"That's not likely," Baker said.

Shauna twisted in her seat to face him. "We're not going in with guns blazing. You told me nobody would get hurt taking the plane, Baker. This is the last time I volunteer for any of your screwball schemes." Shauna pursed her lips and folded her arms.

"It's a little late for backing out now, Munchkin. Maybe a dwarf would, but—"

"Radley Baker, you said you would never, ever call me a—"

"You two need to settle down back there and then settle your dispute. Can't have any explosions taking my Cessna down."

Baker folded his arms across his chest.

It grew silent in the cabin, except for the droning of the engine.

After a few seconds passed, Daggett pointed a thumb over his shoulder at the small backpack Baker had brought with him. "What's in the bag, son?"

"I told you I'm not your son."

"Nope. If you were my son, I'd turn you over my knee and wail the tar outa' you. You should treat the little lady with more respect. You owe her an explanation of how you're gonna get command of a Globemaster. She's worried, Baker."

Baker blew out a blast of frustration and opened the bag that sat beside him. He pulled out an M84. "This is a flashbang grenade. If anyone's by the door, or inside on the cargo floor, we stun them with this. We close the door and we've got command of the ship. Then we get out of Dodge."

"You haven't told me how we even get to the plane without getting shot first."

"Daggett will let us out on the side of the plane opposite the door. C-17's sit so low to the runway that no one on the other side of the plane will see us until we duck under the fuselage and appear suddenly from behind the steps by the doorway."

Shauna looked at the M84 Baker still held in his hand. "One little noisemaker? What if there are people outside the plane **and** inside?"

Baker pulled out his second M84.

"What if the pilot is still in the cockpit?"

"That's enough, Shauna," Baker said. "If you don't want to help me, you can stay with Daggett. I'll do this by myself."

She didn't reply.

"By the way, there will be no pilot in the cockpit. Not until just before takeoff time. I know pilots, Shauna."

"Look, you two need to end the hostilities, pronto. I'm gonna be contacting the Prineville CTAF in a minute or two. It's unmanned, but I don't know for sure what to expect since the military moved in. Regardless, I don't want anyone to know you're onboard."

Shauna slumped in her seat, leaned toward him, and nuzzled her head against his shoulder.

It was a welcome change of mood, but what did it mean?

The droning of the Cessna's engine meant they had to talk loudly to be heard. Shauna had raised her head until her lips touched his ear. Evidently, what was coming was meant to be a private message.

A tear dripped from her cheek and splattered on his bare arm. "I'm sorry, Baker. Really, I am," she whispered.

"If this really frightens you, Shauna, you don't have—"

"Baker I'm only frightened for you, not me."

"I don't understand. I cooked up this scheme because we need to protect our families. Sure it's challenging, but God would have shown me another way if this was foolhardy."

"You're right, you don't understand. Please listen. Whenever I have tried to help someone, something bad always happens. Thinking about the danger ahead, I'm afraid that I've endangered you."

"That's not a rational fear, Munchkin. We can talk about this later."

"We have to talk now. There might not be a later for us."

"If you're talking about some dark moment in your past, that's not rational fear."

"But it is. I had a boyfriend in high school, someone I really cared about. He's dead because of me."

"I'm sorry, Shauna. I don't know the details of your situation from years ago. But I do know that right now, other people's lives are on the line. What we're doing now— this is what I do. It's what I've been trained to do, what I've been called to do. I'm a pilot and a warfighter. You aren't making anything bad happen to me. Only I can do that, and I've already given the outcome of this to God. Now it's time to do my best and trust Him and you for the rest. And I do trust you, Shauna."

"I couldn't forgive myself if anything happened to you today."

"But I could forgive you, because I love you, Shauna Jackson. Besides, whatever happens, it's not your fault."

She kissed his cheek and laid her head on his shoulder.

Dude, just so you know. Whatever's bugging her—it's not over.

Chapter 14

5:00 a.m., Prineville, Oregon

Baker glanced at his watch. 5:00 a.m.. They were supposed to be in Prineville.

Their tight time schedule for the evacuation was being compressed further. They could afford no delays at the Prineville airport.

The radio squawked some static. Daggett must be calling Common Traffic Advisory Frequency, CTAF.

"Prineville Traffic, Cessna four three niner Alpha Bravo, ten miles east of runway, inbound landing, Prineville Traffic," Daggett spoke into the mic.

"Cessna four three niner Alpha Bravo, find another place to land. Prineville is closed."

Daggett practically jumped out of his seat. CTAF was supposed to be automated. "What the—who is monitoring CTAF? You are in violation of FAA procedures."

"Cessna four three niner Alpha Bravo, this is the US Army. Find another place to land."

Daggett muted the mic. "We're troddin' some new sod here, Baker. I'm gonna have to wing it to get us down. Stay quiet. I want them to think it's only me in this bird."

"Got it."

"US Army, Cessna four three niner Alpha Bravo cannot comply. This is an aircraft emergency. I need to land immediately."

In the background multiple voices grew in volume, but Baker couldn't hear all the words. Then the argument seemed to have stopped.

"Cessna four three niner Alpha Bravo, this is Kelly, Manager of the Prineville airport."

"Kelly, finally a voice of reason. I need to land, now."

"Cessna four three niner Alpha Bravo, we have had problems at Prineville with the Army's presence. But I'll work out something to get you on the ground safely."

"Kelly, I would appreciate that. But don't dilly dally. I've got some engine problems."

After a minute of silence, the same army dude came back on. "Cessna four three niner Alpha Bravo, you have permission to land."

Daggett muted the mic. "Baker, I'm gonna land and then taxi to the hanger I use at the south end of the airport. If what I'm seeing ahead is correct, we'll go right by the line of C-17s parked nose-to-tail on the tarmac like a mule train."

"Cessna four three niner Alpha Bravo, use runway thirty-three."

"US Army, cannot comply. I may not make it if I do that. Cessna four three niner Alpha Bravo turning final, runway two-eight, full stop, US Army."

"I'm warning you, Cessna four three niner Alpha Bravo—"

Baker sat up in his seat. "Daggett, you cut him off."

"Your doggone right. I cut the snake off before he could start launchin' threats. I figure that gives us a little more protection. If that viper can't tell us what he might do to us, then he doesn't lose face for not doing it."

Baker shook his head. "More protection you say? I'll have to try that the next time I run into the Taliban in Afghanistan."

"Hang on, you two, we're landing on runway two eight. I'll make it look like an ugly landing to use up all the runway. That makes the shortest path to my hanger go right by those C-17s. Pick out a pretty bird, Baker. I'd suggest the one on the far end. It's parked for a quick getaway."

"Duly noted," Baker said.

There was a light thump of the tires, then the Cessna bounded up into the air again. A second thump on the runway was followed by a third, and finally the little plane was down.

True to Daggett's word, he had used the entire runway.

They made a right turn and began taxiing by the long line of C-17s.

Baker studied Shauna's face. "Are you ready to do this, Munchkin?"

She took his hand and squeezed it. "Ready as I can be."

"I'm gonna slow down like a snail when we're about halfway," Daggett said. "Maybe they'll start to target that point. Then I'll speed up and slow again near the end of the line, so you two can jump out."

"Got it," Baker said.

Baker pointed toward the plane at the head of the line. "Look underneath the plane. The front cargo steps are down, so the door's open. But I see two sets of feet. Stay behind the wheels as we approach, Shauna. They won't be able to see us with the wheels hiding us."

"I'll follow you," Shauna said.

The Cessna slowed its taxi.

"See you later, Daggett."

"Godspeed, you two."

With his small pack on his back, Baker jumped out.

Shauna leaped behind him.

When her feet hit, he caught Shauna before her momentum could send her body sprawling onto the tarmac.

They turned and crept up to the side of the plane using the array of big wheels to hide them.

Baker moved slowly, silently toward the nose of the plane until the steps deployed on the far side hid their legs from view of the two men having a conversation near the base of the steps.

Baker pulled out his handgun and whispered to Shauna. "Keep this ready just in case you need it. There's no safety, just pull the trigger to fire. It works like your Sig Sauer?"

Shauna nodded.

He pulled out an M84 and whispered in her ear. "We crawl under the plane, behind the steps. I'll flashbang them from there. Close your eyes and cover your ears when I throw it. From the time the first grenade goes off, we have to move fast. We'll have maybe sixty seconds until somebody comes to see what's happening."

Shauna nodded.

Baker activated the M84 and gave it a sidearm toss.

It landed behind the two men.

Baker covered up.

Though the steps blocked part of the concussion and light, the explosion thumped against his head like the blow from a large rubber mallet.

He reached for Shauna's hand and tugged.

They circled the steps and ran up them, through the door, and onto the cargo floor.

Two men stood in the cargo area at the base of the cockpit steps.

Baker grabbed and tossed his second M84. "Cover up, Shauna."

Without steps to shield them, this flash and bang hit hard.

Baker turned to check Shauna.

She was shaking her head and appeared a bit wobbly, but she had tucked the gun under the belt of her shorts.

No time to wait for her to shed her grogginess. Baker scooped her up, ran to the cockpit steps, and set her on the bottom step. "As soon as it wears off—"

"It's over. I'm okay."

"Good. Now hurry up the steps to the cockpit area. There should be no one up there. But if you have to shoot, try not to shoot the controls."

She climbed steadily up the steps.

Baker whirled and grabbed one of the unconscious bodies by the ankles, dragged it to the door, and slung it down the steps to the tarmac.

He took the second man by the wrists and drug him to the door.

As Baker slung the man out of the plane, a shot came from the cockpit.

Shauna.

He scrambled up the steps to the cockpit but ran into Shauna who was racing down them.

"There was someone up there. He lunged at me and I—I had to shoot."

"Let me by. I need to check him out." Baker slipped by Shauna and spotted the body of a young man holding his abdomen and groaning.

He approached the man who was only semiconscious. Baker had seen worse wounds in Afghanistan. It wouldn't be fatal provided the guy got medical attention soon.

"He'll live, but I've got to get him out of here."

He dragged the body down the steps and to the front cargo door. "Sorry, dude. He shoved the man and let him tumble down to the tarmac.

Security guards and soldiers in fatigues appeared near one of the buildings fifty or sixty yards to the left.

Baker hit the button to shut the front cargo door of the C-17 and raced to the cockpit.

Shauna stood almost motionless staring at the control panel. "I didn't realize the bullet would go clear through him. I didn't mean to shoot the controls too."

The instrument panel was shattered and blood-splattered in front of the copilot's seat.

Baker studied it for a couple of seconds. "You hit the altimeter and air-speed indicator displays. But don't worry about the controls. The pilot has a full set of instruments, and all of the controls on this bird are quad-redundant with a mechanical backup behind that. It'll fly just fine." He pointed to the seat on the right. "Get in the co-pilot's seat, Shauna. Knees on either side of the stick and buckle in. Then put on that headset."

Baker jumped into the pilot's seat. "The engines are warm and ready to go. That'll save us a lot of time. We're the first plane in the line, so I'm going to get us rolling. But we'll have to take off on 33."

"The small runway?"

"Yes. It's narrow and short, but not nearly as short as McKenzie Bridge State Airport."

Shauna grimaced.

"Don't worry. We'll be fine."

She pointed out the window. "They're raising their guns like they might shoot the plane."

"I think you mean shoot *us*." He hit the thrust lever. The engines screamed, then roared, and the big plane lurched forward.

"They lowered their guns," Shauna said. "But now I can't see them."

"They won't shoot. They can't hit us, and they don't want to damage a bird that cost almost a half billion dollars ... hang on, Shauna. This is a sharp turn onto runway 33."

"Baker ... Baker, you're running off the runway."

"I never did get the hang of making sharp turns with this bird. Using the back thrust is almost as hard as backing up a trailer, except you're moving forward."

"So you did stuff like this in the simulator?"

"Not exactly. I did train on a simulator once at Wright-Patterson Air Force Base. But I also used the video game simulation."

"So I'm flying with a pilot who trained using video games? Just tell me this, Mr. Baker, and I want a straight answer. Can you set this plane down and take off again from that little airfield at McKenzie?"

"Not to worry, Munchkin. Just hold on and I'll show you. Oops!"

Her face snapped around toward him. "That's not a word a passenger wants to hear from their pilot."

"It's okay. We're aligned with the runway now."

"But they're aligning two firetrucks and two Humvees at the other end to stop us. They're driving our way, Baker."

The firetrucks and Humvees raced toward them, two wide and two deep.

"Do they actually think that'll stop me? I can play chicken too, Munchkin. Who do you think's gonna win?"

"You're a gambler, Radley Baker. I didn't think you were that type."

"Sometimes I am. But just so you know, it's not the time yet for this gambler to break even."

The C-17's four engines roared and the plane trembled.

Shauna stopped wiggling as the acceleration pressed them into their seats with its incredible force.

Incredible, but also exhilarating. The invigorating words of an old song popped into his head as the plane roared down the short, narrow runway.

He edited them for the occasion. "She's my C-17. You don't know what I got."

"Baker, I can't believe you're singing while we're strapped onto the biggest suicide bomb in the world."

"This is an airplane, not a bomb."

The C-17's nose rotated upward, and it leaped into the air long before the vehicles racing down the runway reached them.

"Great," Shauna said. "Now we get to be shot down by those Stinger missiles you told me about."

"I told you, they don't want to lose a half-billion-dollar airplane. They're not going to shoot them at us. Within a minute, we'll be beyond their range anyway. They'll only take us down as a last resort. The guys on the ground are probably scheming right now about how they're going to get this bird back."

"What about those Apaches we saw as Daggett taxied down the runway?" Shauna asked.

He didn't want to alarm her about the Apaches, so he didn't reply. But he wondered how Daggett was faring with the questioning about his arrival, which coincided with the pilfering of their plane.

Daggett was quick-witted and had friends at Prineville. He would be okay.

On to the next matter of business. "Shauna, this bird was configured to move troops. It has somewhere around a hundred seats installed near the front of the cargo bay. I need you to check the seats and seat belts and make sure this plane is as ready as it can be to load, seat, and belt in a hundred people. When we start loading them, I'll need you to help expedite getting them seated and buckled in. We won't have any time to spare."

Shauna unbuckled her pilot's belt. "How much time do I have."

"We'll be landing in fifteen minutes, and you need to be in your seat a couple of minutes before that—just before I start my descent."

"You mean before you try to land a C-17 on a postage stamp? I'll be buckled in, Runt. You can count on that."

"You'll be amazed, Munchkin."

"I'll settle for unscathed." She scampered to the steps leading to the cargo area and disappeared.

Their caper hadn't gone exactly as planned, but they were flying away safely and, as far as Baker knew, though four people had been flash-banged and one seriously shot, no one had died.

But Shauna's mentioning the band of hostile Apaches brought worries that **no one dying** was probably going to change. He had other worries about Colonel Craig.

Had Craig and his fifty men been able to hold a force ten times their size?

If not, had Baker and Shauna run out of time to evacuate the women and kids?

Chapter 15

5:00 a.m. McKenzie, Log Cabin Inn

Deke pulled off Highway 126 onto an overgrown driveway that might have once led to a cabin in the woods. But he had picked this spot because a short walk in the woods would take him and his two companions to log cabin number 13.

The resort guide they had downloaded said it slept five. But with two little guys in this group, it had slept six last night, including the unfortunate Ms. Julia Bancroft.

"Babak, Henderson, we're thirty minutes later than I planned. The mountain will shadow this valley for a bit longer, but the twilight is fading fast, so we've got to hurry. And remember, we take everyone in the cabin so there's nobody to sound the alarm."

"We remember the plan, Deke. Let's go. I'm anxious to see the four babes close up," Babak said.

"Babak, seeing is all you get to do. Be sure that your baser proclivities do not interfere with obeying my orders."

Five minutes later, Deke led six zip-tied captives through the woods to his van.

A gun held to the twin boys' heads had so far kept everyone quiet.

At 5:10 a.m., Deke drove north on Highway 126.

In the rearview mirror, Deke watched Babak's eyes rove over the women for the third or fourth time. "I agree, Babak. They are a fine-looking quartet of women, but that is not part of the plan."

"Speaking of the plan," Babak said. "You never did tell us where we're taking them, Deke."

At Babak's last word, Ms. Bancroft's head turned to look at Deke. Their eyes met in the rearview mirror.

Julia Bancroft gasped.

That's right Ms. Weiss, rather Bancroft. It's Deke. Major Nicholas Deke. And I bet you know where I am taking you, don't you?"

Her eyes glared at him defiantly.

But that would change once they got her in the cave.

Ten minutes later, as they approached the intersection with Highway 242, lights flashed and explosions boomed to the north on Highway 126.

"It sounds like the federal troops and the militia are having a friendly little firefight. But we have no time to watch the fireworks." He signaled and turned right onto Highway 242.

Deke had Babak put Julia Bancroft in the middle of the second seat in the van so he could see her in the mirror.

Her eyes had widened when he made the turn onto Highway 242. Evidently, she knew where he was taking her, why he had taken her, and in a general sense what would happen to her there.

The other five in the van were collateral damage. It was unfortunate, because any of the women would have fared well in a beauty pageant, even Ms. Bancroft.

"Deke," Henderson said. "Will Walker still pay us even if we veer off into vengeance mode for a few hours?"

"Don't worry about Walker. I gave him information to set up the ten-to-one slaughter taking place on Highway 126, and I arranged for him to be rid of the Wicked Witch of the West, Sandra Harper, so he can subjugate Oregon, and so I can free my men from where Harper has them incarcerated. It was a clever plan that will get us and Walker exactly what we wanted."

On a straight stretch of road, Deke turned his head and glanced at Julia.

She met his gaze.

"Yes, Ms. Bancroft. Captain Albert Deke was my brother. Wouldn't it be ironic if Ms. Bancroft were to die in the same cave where she killed my brother?"

Chapter 16

5:15 a.m., Highway 126, near Trail Bridge Reservoir

David Craig leaped the guard rail and hugged the tree-lined, rocky bank on the side of Highway 126.

Bullets screamed their complaint as they ricocheted off the pavement and the rocks along the roadway.

The militia had met the enemy a quarter of a mile south of Trail Bridge Reservoir.

Craig had wanted to reach the reservoir, where he would only have to defend one flank, because the reservoir bordered the west side of the highway. But he could be thankful the sentry posted at Lost Lake Creek had warned him earlier that the Stryker Brigade was turning from Highway 20 onto Highway 126, headed south toward McKenzie.

A reckless drive around the South Sister, well above the speed limit, had allowed him to reach the intersection of Highways 126 and 242, cutting off the brigade from McKenzie where the families were waiting to be evacuated.

The one JLTV that hadn't needed any maintenance should arrive any time now. JLTVs, with a top speed of seventy, couldn't keep up with their other vehicles' highway speeds. But the armored vehicle, with missiles and a chain gun, could be key in keeping Stryker Brigade from overrunning his militia platoon.

Now, to hold the brigade here for forty-five minutes, until 0545, when Baker would evacuate the women and kids from the airfield only ten miles to the south. Craig would sacrifice himself and all fifty of his men, if necessary, to make that happen.

The militia had two SMAWs. These were powerful RPGs that shot thermobaric rockets which could destroy a truck, a Humvee full of men, or even an entire house. One explosion from a thermobaric rocket could stop a company of charging men.

Craig cupped a hand around his mouth. "Drew!"

"Yes, sir!"

"Take two men and one of the SMAWs and move 200 yards up the road, in the trees. Cover our right flank ... Scotty!"

"Yes, sir!"

"Take two men and our other SMAW and move 200 yards up the road to cover our left flank. Both of you come back when you run out of rockets."

Both responded and quickly selected their trio of men, grabbed their weapons and rockets, then disappeared into the forest on either side of the road.

If only he had an update on Baker's status, then Craig could plan more precisely how to allocate his meager resources. For now, he would rely heavily on the firepower of the JLTV, both its missiles and its M230 chain gun.

Smith, JLTV commander, stuck his head out the driver's door. "Here they come, Colonel. Looks like an all-out assault to overrun us."

"Give them everything you've got, Smith. We have to stop them. Men! Use the rocks and the JLTV for cover. When I give the order, fire at will. But be aware we have three of our men guarding our flanks on either side about two hundred yards ahead."

Craig waited until the wall of charging men reached a point a hundred yards ahead. "Fire at will!"

The valley echoed with booms of Hellfire missiles launched from the JLTV, the staccato rattling of its chain gun, and the sound of M4 rifle fire.

As quickly as they had advanced, the brigade retreated.

The boom and rocket explosions produced by the SMAWs sounded from both sides of the road.

Smith stuck his head out again. "They were just probing us, Colonel Craig."

"Yes. Trying to divert attention so they could attack us from our flanks. But it sounded like Drew and Scotty sent them running back to the reservoir."

Craig's sat phone went off. "The caller ID indicated Kingsley Air Force Base. Great! Why couldn't they have called fifteen minutes ago?

Drew and his men scurried out of the forest on the left.

In a couple more seconds, Scotty and his men approached from the right.

Drew was breathing hard. "Sir, we were nearly overrun, but gave them our three rockets and a lot of rifle fire. After we took out about thirty men, they retreated."

"How many did they send your way?" Craig said.

"I'd say a hundred. Maybe a hundred and fifty."

"Same thing over on the right," Scotty said. "We got twenty-five or thirty of them."

Craig whistled through his teeth. "They meant to wipe us out by sending nearly 300 men hitting us on our flanks. Thanks, men. You saved us for the time being. But, Drew, what's your guess about their next move?"

"They evidently want this to end quickly so they can move on to McKenzie. They'll mount a charge straight down this highway with everything they've got and try to blast through our line."

"My thoughts exactly," Craig said. "I just had a call from Kingsley command post. I didn't have time to pick it up. I'll return it now and ask for CAS. Are you guys ready for some help from above?"

'Bring on the Eagles," Drew said.

"But tell them to hurry," Scotty added. "The way it looks, we may need them in ten minutes or so."

"Yeah. I agree." Craig returned the call.

"Major Shablow, Kingsley command post here. Is that you, Craig?"

"Yes. Here's our position." Craig sent him the GPS coordinates in a message. "And we need CAS ASAP. We held off Stryker Brigade's first charge. But we've only got fifty men with rifles, the chain gun on our JLTV, and maybe one missile left. They're going to charge us with over four hundred men. They'll have RPGs and other nice little gifts for us. How quickly can you get here?"

"Craig ..." Shablow's voice dropped in volume and went monotone. This couldn't be good news.

"What's happening, Shablow?"

"We just received word that all the Apaches left Prineville."

Not good. "Can't you intercept them and take them all down?"

"It's not going to be that easy. They all took different routes to—well, we don't know how many destinations. They could target your homes, your dependents, and/or your battle near Trail Bridge Reservoir."

Shablow knew Craig's location. "So you looked up our coordinates?"

"Yes, sir. I did."

"Shablow, can you cover our battle area with half of your Eagles and then our families' location with the rest and take out any incoming Apaches before they arrive?"

"That's why I called you to get your position and your status. Where are your dependents located?"

Craig had allied his forces with the Oregon Air Guard, but thoughts of a traitor or a spy among them niggled. But surely, he could trust a commander of the fighter wing with the women's and kids' location. "Our people are in two resorts at the town of McKenzie, but they will soon be boarding a C-17 at the McKenzie Bridge State Airport."

"The McKenzie airfield? You're kidding me, right?"

"That's right. No kidding."

"Is this a test of my competence or something? And how did the militia get a C-17?"

"Just like we got our JLTVs and our Chinooks. We stole—let me rephrase that. We **acquired** them, Major Shablow, from the folks at JBLM who were using them to kill us. By the way, have you heard from Captain Baker?"

"Uh ... just a minute."

"I don't have a minute. We need CAS, now!"

The other end went silent.

Drew leaned in close. "Sir, it looks like they're about ready to charge. We might be able to hold off the first charge. But after that, it doesn't look good."

"Prepare the men for an orderly retreat down the highway. First give them all the heavy ordinance we have left. It will stop them. Then use the chain gun to eliminate any Humvees that you see. After that, each retreat will be preceded with intense rifle fire and a burst from the M230."

"Got it, sir."

Thoughts of Susan leading the evacuation of wives and kids played through his mind. Was she safe? Were all the dependents safe?

"Colonel Craig?" Shablow was back on the line.

Craig needed to get his head in the current battle with Stryker Brigade or none of the rest mattered. "Craig here. So what did you find out?"

"Someone tried to contact us a while ago. We thought it was some kook or a diversionary tactic by the federal troops. We cut him off."

"You need to let him in on that frequency, Shablow. He's picking up our civilians and taking them to your base. I can't contact him while he's in the air, and I need his status to time our retreat."

"You're retreating?"

Craig snipped the word, **duh**, from the tip of his tongue. "Of course we're retreating. We're fifty against nearly five hundred, and we're running low on ammo. That's why we need CAS. If our ammo gets too low, we'll be overrun."

"Scrambling all our available Eagle's now, Craig. You know that for normal operations CAS would be command-controlled from Camp Rilea, don't you?"

"Yes, we talked about that, but since our activity will be mostly in Eastern Oregon, we decided to bypass Rilea unless the war moved to Western Oregon. That's why I called you, Shablow."

"Just letting you know."

"Did you learn anything else from Baker?"

"Whoever it was that called in was flying a C-17, and he told us a story similar to yours."

"So you believe **me** and not **him**?"

"Colonel Craig, let's just say you corroborated his story. But no one lands at Kingsley unless we know they are on our side. I've still got to brief all my people about it so no one gets hurt."

"And I've got to go." Craig said. "We're about to come under heavy fire from an attack. How long until those Eagles arrive?"

"About ten more minutes."

"Call me when they need exact coordinates. But remember, we'll be slowly retreating southward, while the enemy advances toward us. The target should be clearly visible from the air. If not, call me to verify our position before those Eagles start launching any missiles or guided bombs."

"Will do, Craig. Since we anticipated CAS, each Eagle is carrying six AGM-65 Maverick missiles. Combine those with their gatling gun and they should wreak havoc on the federal forces. We sent out four F-15s equipped with AIM-120Ds to take down those Apaches, and they can do that from a hundred miles away. Forget I said that, Craig. It's classified info."

"Forgot it already. Don't let those Apaches near us or our civilians. Gotta run, Shablow. But I can't wait for the fireworks show to begin, sponsored by the Eagles."

"Here they come, Craig." Drew raised his M4 to the ready position.

"Scotty!"

From the gunner's seat, Scotty rose and stuck his head out of the JLTV.

"Use the last Hellfire Missile to stop the leading edge of the charge. Use the M230 to destroy any Humvee that comes our way, and then mow down the troops until they retreat. It shouldn't take long."

Scotty waved to Craig, then ducked back in the JLTV and closed the door.

"Ready, men!" Craig scanned his troops. They were ready. "Fire at will."

A large boom was quickly followed by a massive ball of flame. Two Humvees and a platoon of men were engulfed in it. Then the chain gun cut loose.

The carnage was widespread and sickening, especially to realize they were doing this to American troops. And knowing that these troops were following unconstitutional orders didn't help the sick feeling in Craig's gut.

The charge ended with sporadic rifle fire from the militia's M4s. Altogether in this charge, the militia appeared to have eliminated or incapacitated another hundred federal troops. They were now down to a little over three hundred.

A roar echoed through the river valley as two F-15s popped up over a ridge to the south.

The arrangement of troops on the battlefield was very clear and the militia hadn't moved since giving their coordinates to the command post.

Craig wasn't surprised when, with no further communications, the Eagles launched four missiles at the enemy. Unleashed upon a narrow column of men crowded onto the highway, the missiles' destruction was incredible.

At least another hundred men met their maker in that moment. The Stryker Brigade was now down to about two hundred men, and for the moment, they were retreating.

A roar came from the distance to the south, the roar of reverse thrusters.

Baker was trying to land.

The militia had prevented Stryker Brigade from interfering with loading the women and children. But what about the incoming Apaches?

Chapter 17

5:40 a.m., at 10,000 feet, near McKenzie Bridge State Airport

Shauna scrambled up the steps into the cockpit of the big C-17. She took the copilot's seat beside Baker and slipped on her headset. "All of the seats are ready. But if my count is correct, even using the two extra seats in here, we're six seats short of seating everyone."

Baker shook his head. "Everybody has to be belted in. Who knows what we might encounter taking off or enroute? We're starting our descent into McKenzie. You need to fasten your belt too, Munchkin."

She slid into the harness and buckled in. "What are we going to do?"

"Some of the younger kids may get buckled in with their moms. It's only a twenty-five-minute trip to Kingsley in this bird." He pointed ahead to their right. "We've been descending for the last three or four minutes. See the airfield?"

She strained to focus on the faint green stripe.

This was not possible. Not even for Baker. "You mean this plane is gonna land on that little green stripe painted on the forest?"

"Oh ye of little faith. This incredible piece of engineering is going to do the inverse of what it did when we took off on the small runway at Prineville."

"Got any parachutes?"

"I doubt it. Paratroopers bring theirs with them. Pilots are supposed to land their birds, not abandon them."

She couldn't take her eyes off the tiny landing strip. "At least it's getting a little bigger."

"It's still 2,600 feet long, Munchkin. It will look more inviting when we get a little closer."

"Inviting? Inviting us to a smoking hole party."

Now the forest trees rushed at them, but the runway was still up ahead.

Baker's hands worked the controls and the engines roared as the big plane vibrated. But they were slowing.

Didn't airplanes stall when they flew this slow? Didn't they fall out of the sky and crash?"

The roaring turned to a thundering that reverberated in her chest.

She couldn't look at the danger zooming at them. Instead she studied Baker's face.

His gaze was locked on the runway. No signs of panic, only of concentration.

The big plane cleared the trees and thumped on the grassy sod.

As the roar grew still louder, an unseen force threw Shauna's body forward against the straps around her. It held her against the straps as the trees at the far end of the runway raced toward them.

Finally, the big plane decelerated to taxiing speed. The trees were still two or three hundred yards ahead. Baker had done it.

Shauna looked across at him. "Baker, that was ... absolutely—"

"Incredible?" He grinned at her. "Munchkin, this plane practically flies itself, and it tells me nearly everything I need to do."

She took a deep breath and let it out slowly, trying to slow her galloping heart.

The plane came to a complete stop at the end of the grass.

"Now to turn this baby around." Baker worked the controls.

The engines on the right sounded much louder than the two on the left. But the mammoth jet slowly spun around in place.

After completing the turn, Baker slowed the engines to something like an idle.

Shauna scanned the runway on the right, the side nearest the highway.

About three hundred yards away a group of people hurried toward the C-17. Mostly moms with kids in tow.

Baker unbuckled his harness. "Let's load them through the front door."

Shauna beat him to the steps and scrambled down them to open the door.

By the time the steps came to rest on the ground, Susan stood at the base of the steps. The taut lines on her face tied a knot in Shauna's stomach.

They were about to be rescued. There should only be good news and hope at this point.

Shauna scampered down the steps.

Baker's bootsteps sounded right behind her.

She stopped in front of Susan and tried to lay a hand on her shoulder, but Susan appeared so distraught that her shoulder was a moving target. "Susan, what's wrong?"

"You need to tell us quickly," Baker said. "We've got to get all of your people out of here in five minutes."

Susan wiped a tear from one cheek. "That's not possible. Not for some of us. We're missing six. Everyone that was in Julia's cabin is gone."

"What?" Shauna said.

"What?" Baker echoed.

"When they didn't show up to load up their things, we checked on them. The cabin door was unlocked, and it stood open. All their things were in the room except them.

They were taken, most likely in their pajamas, and we think they're wearing their shoes. We threw their things in Julia's SUV and drove it over here with the other vehicles."

"Susan, we don't have time to—" Baker's phone rang.

He pulled it out of his phone pocket. "It's Craig. I've got to answer. Shauna, start seating everyone."

Shauna motioned the group that had gathered around them to climb up the steps.

After she showed Susan how to use the military seatbelts, Susan took over seating the women and kids.

"I thought we would have to double up some kids with their moms," Shauna said. "But since we're down six, we should just fit. I'm gonna go back outside to see what Baker found out from Craig."

Susan nodded. Her earlier agitation seemed to have subsided now that she had something to do to help.

A picture had been forming in Shauna's mind since she heard about the likely abduction of Julia and those in her cabin. It wasn't a good picture.

She hurried down the steps to where Baker paced back and forth with his phone to his ear.

By the time she reached him, he was putting his phone away. The look on his face wasn't much different from Susan's when she arrived.

"What's wrong, Baker?"

"Craig says he thinks the militia has stopped Stryker Brigade, but they launched all of the Apaches from Prineville. Kingsley sent four Eagles to hunt them down, but the fifteen Apaches all took different routes. If one were to get through, we could—"

"How soon might they get here?"

"We think they took off about fifteen minutes after we stole the C-17. At top speed, on a direct flight, one or more Apaches could reach us by six o'clock. Their AIM missiles travel at over 1800 miles-per-hour and have a range of about twenty miles, though they have hit targets farther away than that."

"Baker, we need to be in the air at six o'clock if we're gonna stay out of their range."

"Shauna ... did Susan say who was in the cabin with Julia."

She nodded. "The other five were Itzy, Kathy, Gemma, and the twins, Josh and Caleb."

Baker shook his head. "Steve could lose his whole family. And Julia's pregnant."

"We can't let that happen." The heat on her neck and cheeks turned to a raging fire. "I think I know who took them and where they're going. And I've got to stop them!"

"*You've* got to stop them? Shauna, we've got to fly the families to Kingsley before we do anything."

"Correction, *you* have got to fly them to Kingsley. Julia and the others might all be dead before we could get back. But not if I hurry."

"Out with it, Munchkin. Hurry to where?"

"Don't you remember what Julia told us at the meeting that night a couple of weeks ago? The story about a man named Deke?"

"Sort of. Refresh my memory."

"Julia told us she killed a man named Deke nine years ago when President Hannan sent a black ops team to kill them. It happened in the Skylight Cave. I think this is Deke's brother and he has some perverted desire for revenge. That's where he will take them. I've got Siggie in my holster, I can get Julia's car keys from Susan."

"No, Shauna! I forbid—"

"Sorry, Baker, I've got to go, and you need to take off. If I don't make it back in a few hours, you'll know where to find me."

She ran up the steps to Susan's seat on the plane. "I need Julia's car keys."

"They're in her SUV, under the floor mat. But why?"

"Baker can fill you in on that later." She sprinted down the steps and collided with Baker on the bottom step.

She sidestepped him and continued running across the runway toward the parked cars.

"Shauna, come back!"

She didn't stop. Couldn't stop.

"Munchkin!"

She needed to say something. Shauna turned her head and yelled. "Goodbye, Baker! Pray for me!"

Chapter 18

Baker had seen Shauna a couple of times before when she set her mind on something, and he remembered once when she had tried to set someone else's mind on something. In either case, there was no stopping her.

And the truth be told, someone had to stop what might be going down in that Skylight Cave. He just didn't want it to be her—Munchkin versus the monster, a blood avenger.

Baker couldn't dwell on the danger to Shauna while he held the lives of nearly a hundred people in his hands. He needed to get them safely to Kingsley Air Force Base, then he could think about helping Shauna.

He sensed movement behind him, and he looked back toward the steps.

Susan approached tentatively and took the co-pilot's seat. "What is Shauna up to? Is she going to be safe?"

"She thinks she's going to rescue Julia and the others."

"Baker, does Shauna know where they are?"

"According to Shauna, Deke took Julia and the other five to the Skylight Cave."

"The Skylight Cave? How does she know that?"

He didn't have time for this. "Susan, fifteen Apaches were sent from Prineville to take this plane down. We've got to leave now."

"I thought Craig had stopped the attack."

"He stopped the ground assault. Now someone, probably Walker, wants to strike a demoralizing blow by killing our families. That man's a demon."

"Is there anything I can do to help?"

"Yes. Go tell everyone to buckle in and that we're going to takeoff now. Tell them it will be very loud and might feel like a carnival ride when we lift off. Put somebody in charge back there, maybe Beth or AJ. Come back when you're done, and I'll answer your questions if I have time."

Susan hurried across the cabin to the steps.

Baker turned his attention to the displays and then reached overhead to make the adjustments needed to ready the plane for takeoff.

Susan reappeared and slid into the co-pilot's seat.

"Buckle in, Susan, and pray that I can get this bird configured for an austere runway takeoff."

She straddled the stick and began buckling in. "Just how austere is this runway?"

The engines began to whine at a higher pitch.

"Normally, with a C-17 we're wrestling with landing on a short runway while carrying a full load and then trying to stop in time. Landing was no problem. But now we're taking off with a hundred more people. Don't worry, though. With those four big Pratt and Whitney engines and high-lift wings, this bird can practically leap into the air."

The engines' whine turned to a roar as Baker used reverse thrust to back up to the very end of the runway. He would use all 2,600 feet to ensure the takeoff was safe.

The engines' thunderous sound made normal conversation impossible. Baker pointed at the headset now in Susan's lap and then pointed at her head.

Susan nodded and slipped it on.

He glanced at his watch. 0605. The episode with Shauna had cost them precious time. Hopefully, the Apaches modified routes, trying to disguise their targets, would add minutes to their arrival time.

"Time to go." Baker glanced at Susan.

He pushed the yoke forward and the engines thundered out their full-power voices in four-part harmony.

The big plane started its assault on the short runway.

The fuselage trembled at what was coming.

Maybe it was Baker's insides trembling. He'd never taken off under duress with such a precious cargo.

While the acceleration pressed him back in his seat, the trees at the far end of the runway rushed at him at an incredible rate. Baker glanced at the speed, shot a prayer heavenward, and pulled on the yoke.

The C-17 tilted upward.

Blue sky filled the front windows.

By the time he craned his neck to see the trees below, they were far below.

No stall warnings.

The big cargo plane had performed incredibly.

"Are we doing okay?" Susan looked his way.

"More than okay. We're—"

A warning sounded in the cockpit.

Bright flashes on the radar warning receiver grabbed his attention.

Words formed on the display. Baker focused on them, especially the word **missile**.

He could not let his passengers down. Radley Baker would not be the be the man who forced recovery teams to search these mountains for the bodies of children.

Baker glanced at the radar display and saw the menacing object approaching. "Hang on, Susan. They shot a missile at us."

"Who's they?"

"An Apache about thirty miles to the northwest. It's a long shot for that missile, but he probably knew we would quickly run away from his bird if he waited."

"When, Baker?"

"In about twenty seconds."

"Can we run away from it, or do I say my final prayer?"

"It travels a over 1,800 miles-per-hour. We can't outrun it. But in about ten seconds, we should see our counter measures deploy ... there goes one."

A bright flash came from behind, lighting the cockpit with a bluish-white light.

Baker banked to the right, extending the distance from the incoming missile and moving out of its path.

"Are we okay now, Baker?"

"Yes. No. Doggone!"

"Doggone what!"

"No. We're not okay. They launched another one."

Another flare deployed as the second missile bore down on them.

Baker banked left this time.

The flare's bright light came accompanied by another flash of light.

A concussion hit the C-17 like the blow from a giant hammer. It created an earthquake in the cockpit.

"Did it hit us?" Susan's blue eyes had widened considerably.

"No." Baker cranked the throttle wide open.

The engines rumbled their response.

"Our countermeasures worked. They haven't launched another missile, but if they do, it will die chasing us. We're out of range now, Susan."

"I guess I didn't need that final prayer after all."

"Out of curiosity, what does a final prayer include? Would it mention David Craig?"

"None of your business, Baker."

"You're right." He paused. "In a couple of minutes, if there are no more threats, I need you to go and check on the others. Let them know what happened and that we're safe."

"I wonder if they were praying as hard as I was."

Baker backed off slightly on the throttle. "They might not have known anything was happening except for me banking twice and the one explosion. You can't see anything down there in the cargo area." He paused. "I think we're good to go. I need to call Kingsley now."

"Then I'll go check on the women and the kids."

Baker took in a deep breath and let it out slowly. This could get dicey. Hopefully, Kingsley had been briefed on their arrival and would be cooperative. If not ...

"Kingsley Tower, Militia C-17 declaring an aircraft emergency. Requesting to land with a load of women and children." It sounded hokey, but he'd put the words out there and they were the truth.

"C-17, Kingsley Tower. What kind of fool do you take me for? Permission to land refused. If you proceed, you will be shot down. By the way who are you, Mr. Pilot?"

"Who are you, sir?"

"If you're a pilot, it's not sir. This is Sergeant Fox and ... uh, here comes my boss."

"This is Major Grieve at Kingsley tower. Who the heck are you, and what's in that C-17 that you want to set down on my runway? Have you got a load of Rangers waiting to make an assault on our base?"

"Sir, I'm Captain Baker, a member of the Central Oregon Militia. I'm one of their pilots."

"Baker sounds familiar, but the militia doesn't have any C-17s or C-17 pilots."

"They do now, sir."

"What's the tail number on that bird, and how did the militia get a C-17?"

"Don't know the tail number, sir."

"What do you mean you don't know? You're flying the consarned cargo jet."

"I stole it from JBLM's Ranger deployment that's now in Prineville."

"You stole it. How clever. Don't look now, Captain Baker, but two Eagles are sitting by the runway with missiles aimed at your touch down point and there's another Eagle on your tail with the pilot's finger on the missile launcher."

Baker started his descent.

"Look, Major Grieve, I've only got women and children onboard. They're frightened and were almost killed today. These are the families of the Oregon Militia. We used countermeasures for a couple of incoming AIMs, so I need to land to check for damage."

"To make sure this base is safe, I either have to shoot you down or run you off. Which is it going to be Captain Baker?"

"You do what you think is best, sir, but you'll have to live with it. I'm proceeding with landing."

Silence on the other end.

Baker waited and continued his descent with an Eagle glued to his tail.

"Okay, you land, Baker. But stop at the far end of the runway where our Eagles will keep their AGM-65 Maverick Missiles on you while your *women and children* file out. If anything looks suspicious, I'll give the order to send you on a one-way trip to Hades."

"Major, you can't do that."

"You *don't* say."

"I *do say*, sir. Nearly everyone on this plane is a Christian."

Muffled cursing came through the speaker.

"Major, I hope you won't use that language in front of these kids. These are some of the most patriotic and exceptional families in the state. Please, don't hurt them."

"Would that mean certain nine-year-old twins are onboard?"

"Josh and Caleb aren't here, major. But if they were, I'd suggest that you not threaten them. Most who do that haven't survived."

"Baker?" It was a new voice, and it came with authority.

"Baker here. To whom am I speaking?"

"This is Major Shablow at the command post. Major Grieve was not fully briefed on your, uh, mission. Go ahead and land but follow his instructions. It will go a lot more smoothly if you do."

"Thanks, major. Ready to follow instructions right after I land this bird."

Baker lined up with the runway and made his approach. After the antagonistic welcome he'd received, he was tempted to showboat by way of an austere runway landing, but the passengers had been through enough today.

He set the C-17 down softly and used most of the runway to decelerate.

Baker stopped the big jet at the end of the runway, cut the engines, unbuckled, and walked toward the cargo area. He stopped at the head of the steps leading down to where the women and kids sat. "We're on the ground at Kingsley and I'm going to open the doors in a minute. But they're a little leery of a strange C-17 landing on their runway, so I need you to file out of here in an orderly, non-threatening manner. There are two F-15s pointing their Maverick Missiles at us right now. We don't want to provoke them. Do you all understand?"

Heads nodded throughout the cargo hold.

"All right. Let's go, everyone."

Baker descended the short stairway to the cargo hold, opened the front door, and lowered the steps.

Two Humvees raced down the runway looking prickly with all the rifle barrels poking out of them.

"Okay, folks, remember to move slowly and follow all directions that they give us. They mean us no harm. They're just being cautious."

He turned toward Susan who stood behind him near the open door. "Come with me, Susan. Let me do the introductions to break the ice."

"After what that major said, don't you mean to douse the blazes?"

"That too."

The first Humvee stopped, and a young first lieutenant stepped off the vehicle and studied Baker and Susan for a moment. "I'm Lieutenant Howard, Kingsley Security Police."

"And I'm Captain Radley Baker." He turned toward Susan. "And this is Susan O'Connell, Colonel David Craig's fiancé."

"Colonel Craig. That's a name I recognize. Ms. O'Connell, glad to meet you." He turned back toward Baker. "In a couple of minutes, we'll send two buses out to take the civilians to a safe place. There will be some questions and then we'll decide what to do with you all."

***

While they waited for the buses, Susan pulled out her cell phone. "We need to call David and let him know our status. Who got here safely and who didn't."

Baker nodded.

She placed the call and turned on her speaker phone.

"Susan, when I called before we took off, I didn't get a chance to tell Craig about our missing people and Shauna's escapade. I didn't even know who was missing at the time. Tell him who's missing and that we need a plan to go help Shauna."

Craig answered on the second ring. "Craig, here. Is that you, Susan?"

"Yes. We're at Kingsley, but we need to tell you what happened before we took off from McKenzie."

Baker listened as Susan recounted finding six people kidnapped, Shauna's suspicion that it was Deke's doing, and then Shauna's attempt to find them at Skylight Cave.

"How long ago did you take off?"

"About forty-five minutes," Susan said.

"That's about how long it would take Shauna to drive to the cave if she hurried," Craig said.

"She hurried all right," Baker said. "She hit the pavement with the tires squealing."

"Is that you, Baker?"

"Yes, sir."

"Does she know the way to the cave?" Craig asked.

"Yeah. She was there with our group less than two weeks ago." Baker said. "She's good with directions. She'll drive straight to it."

"I have some info I need to pass to you, Baker," Craig said. "But Kate needs to hear this too. Susan, can you patch her into this call?"

"Give me a minute to call her."

Susan set up the three-way call.

"Susan said you wanted to talk to me." Kate's voice.

"Kate, I just got a call from State Police Special Operations Commander, Major James Sellers. A mysterious special operations force attacked Mahonia Hall and abducted your aunt."

From Kate's breath, a blast of static came through the phone. "How, Craig? She doubled her security guard."

"We think they infiltrated it."

"What do you think they plan to do with her?"

"There haven't been any **ransom** calls yet, but we think they might want to use her to free the men she put in the state prison. Some of the prisoners are members of Deke's old black ops team."

"How can we be sure they won't harm her after she frees Deke's men?"

"We can't be sure, but knowing the woman your aunt has demonstrated herself to be, she won't free them regardless of what they threaten to do to her."

"You're not painting a very promising picture, Craig. What are we going to do? Let them kill her?"

"No. But we might **force** them to kill her if we go charging in."

"Do the State Police know where she is?"

"The kidnappers are leaving Western Oregon and trying to come east, toward Santiam Pass, probably to link up with the Stryker Brigade for protection."

"We'll never get her back if they join with the brigade."

"Maybe. Though the brigade is in full retreat, the kidnappers could still try to join them. But I've got an idea."

Chapter 19

6:15 a.m., Highway 242

Shauna slowed the SUV from eighty miles-per-hour down to sixty-five on the narrow, two-lane highway that skirted Mount Washington.

From McKenzie, there were two routes to the Skylight Cave. Stryker Brigade would come down Highway 126 to McKenzie if Craig couldn't stop them, so she chose Highway 242 to avoid hostile troops on her way to the cave. That would keep a mountain between her and the troops. But she needed to arrive in one piece if she was to have any chance of rescuing her six friends that Deke had abducted.

She hit the brake pedal and slowed to sixty-five.

But if Deke carried out his plan before she arrived, they would all be dead.

Shauna punched the gas pedal and didn't back off until the speedometer hit ninety.

You've never been able to pull your weight with the militia, girl. What makes you think that all by yourself you can stop a group of trained special forces?

Since she was a young girl, Shauna had always been too small and insignificant to matter. Though she was a good athlete, she was always near the last to be picked when sides were chosen for games.

The accusing voice inside was right. She couldn't contribute at all. Certainly not like Baker. Maybe that's why their relationship had been running like a slow-motion replay.

What did Baker really think about her? That she was a munchkin, so weak that he had to protect her?

She flew by a roadside sign pointing up the mountain. That was Dee Wright Observatory.

If she remembered correctly, the forest service road to the cave was about seven or eight minutes ahead. Probably less at speeds averaging eighty miles-per-hour.

The high, steep bank on her left slowly shrank as she left the shoulder of the mountain and headed toward flatter land to the east.

What was the forest service road they took to the cave? NF1026 or NF1028? There had been a sharp turn in the highway near this National Forest Road. Maybe the turn would help her find it.

Shauna slowed when she saw a turn ahead. To her left a dirt road headed north into a sparse, scrubby pine forest. The sign said NF1028.

This had to be the one.

She turned onto it and drove at thirty miles-per-hour leaving a cloud of red dust in the SUV's wake.

The cave lay somewhere to the east of her position on NF1028, but the road she was on only ran northward as far as she could see.

The road forked unexpectedly.

Shauna jerked the steering wheel to the right. But the right fork didn't turn eastward. It continued to the north.

In a few more seconds, a crossroad came into view. It ran east-west.

Shauna turned right and slowed.

Lava outcroppings separated by stands of pine trees dotted the land. This landscape looked familiar. The cave must be nearby.

She slowed to ten miles-per-hour. That eliminated her dust cloud and most of the vehicle noise.

A hundred yards ahead, a narrow road, not much more than a trail, cut southward through a sparse pine forest. This was the road that led to the cave.

She parked the car, hiding it as best she could behind a patch of pine saplings.

As she slid out of Julia's SUV, Shauna ran her hand under her tank top to the small of her back. She curled her fingers around the grip of her Sig Sauer.

She trusted God but could not deny that feeling the powerful weapon had calmed her and given her confidence.

For now, she would keep her gun hidden behind her.

Shauna crept slowly along a lava rock protrusion. It ran for more than a hundred yards ahead. It also formed the ceiling to the Skylight Cave.

What was going on underneath the ground, thirty feet below her?

If she wanted an answer to that question, from here on, she needed to make every move silently and with caution. If she gave herself away, not only could she be killed, but Julia, Itzy, Gemma, the twins, and Kathy Gore would have no chance. Deke would kill them all.

Faintly, from somewhere ahead, came the sound of a voice—harsh, angry, and threatening. It wasn't difficult to imagine that voice coming from Satan himself.

Chapter 20

0630, near the intersection of Highways 242 and 126

Craig rode shotgun beside Drew in the Humvee they had **acquired** from the retreating remnants of the defeated brigade.

He pulled out his cell from its pocket in his fatigues and spun it around with his fingers. "From what Baker said, I'm guessing that Shauna could be arriving at the cave about now."

"We need to be in two places at once, chasing down the government's kidnappers and helping Shauna free six of our people at the Skylight Cave," Drew said.

"Shauna's smart, but she's going to be outnumbered by several special force types, trained thugs like Deke. If she tries anything, she won't last an hour before they capture or kill her."

Drew nodded and braked for a turn in the road. "And in another hour, the kidnappers will catch up to what's left of Stryker Brigade and join them. If they do, we might never again see Governor Harper alive."

Craig hit the speed dial number for Steve's sat phone. "I'm going to pull Steve's forces back from guarding the cities and the ranch to help us out here."

He answered on the first ring. "Steve here, Colonel Craig. I was just about to call you."

"We need your help out here. Post some sentries near town and by the ranch then move your men into position behind Stryker Brigade after they get on Highway 20. That should put you between Harper's kidnappers and the brigade troops."

"Should I bring my men in right behind the troops to provide a little incentive for them to keep moving toward Prineville?"

"Yes. Your force is twice the size of theirs. That will dispel any notion of them going after our people at the ranch or in Redmond. Then I'm—"

"You're going to the Skylight Cave, aren't you?"

"Yes."

"But I know that cave better than you, Craig, and my wife is in there."

"That's all the more reason for you **not** to go. You couldn't be objective."

"I've been in tight places before with Julia, and I always got her out safely. Come on, Captain Craig! I need to be there."

"So I've been demoted to captain? Steve, **Captain Craig** was quite a few years ago. See what I mean."

He paused. "Drew and I will go. We need you to let us do our job while you do yours. Once you're sure Stryker is going to Prineville, then you can turn around to stop the team that has the governor. By then we should be done at the Skylight Cave and can slip in behind them. We'll have the kidnappers surrounded. But if we're late in arriving and you have to engage them, you must keep Sandra Harper alive."

"It'll become a hostage situation when they threaten to kill her."

"I know. So you stall, negotiate, offer to give them whatever they ask for within reason. She's their only bargaining chip. They will only cash her in as a last resort."

"Yes, sir." Steve's voice had lost its usual enthusiasm.

"If you must engage them, be careful, because we don't know who is in the black ops team that took Governor

Harper, but I'm guessing President Walker hand-picked those men."

"We'll be careful, sir."

As Craig ended the call, a small plane flew by them on their left. It dipped its wings, waving at them, then headed south and slowly descended. It was going to land at McKenzie Bridge airstrip.

"Drew, do you think that's Daggett?"

"I'm not sure, sir."

"We don't have any time to waste."

Drew accelerated to well above the speed limit. "If that's Daggett, we can save a lot of time."

"I'll call Baker. He's still at Kingsley." He hit Baker's number.

"Baker here."

"This is Craig. We're near the McKenzie airfield and we think Daggett just landed there. What is he flying?"

"Daggett's bird is a blue and white Cessna 150."

"It was Daggett. We're going to see if he can get us close to the Skylight Cave."

"Sir, remember Munchkin is headed there too. Daggett can put you down right on it, sir, but I wouldn't recommend that." Baker paused. "What should I do with this stolen C-17."

"It's not stolen. It's acquired equipment," Craig said. "Stay there and see if you can find somebody qualified to fly it."

"So I'm supposed to give it away?"

"I didn't say that. Just look for a pilot. I'm not giving you any orders, Baker. If you find a pilot, I'm sure you'll figure out what to do with the plane." Craig ended the call.

Drew raised his eyebrows. "So you and I are going spelunking?"

"Something like that. Have you ever rescued anyone from a cave, Drew?"

"No but I rescued someone from a box canyon with a wildfire chasing us."

"That's close enough for government work. Let's get to McKenzie Airfield. I've got a proposal for Daggett."

Chapter 21

Nearly 7:00 a.m., Skylight Cave

Clad in pajamas and shoes, Josh James sat beside his twin brother Caleb near the first skylight in the big lava tube known as the Skylight Cave.

The rock floor was only smooth in places. Most of it had jagged lava outcroppings and lava rocks that had fallen from the ceiling of the cave at least thirty feet above them.

Three special forces soldiers had lined up the six captives—Julia, Itzy, Kathy Gore, Gemma, Josh and Caleb—along the cave wall, all sitting on the cave floor in their pajamas.

Now the man called Henderson was approaching Josh and Caleb with zip ties and a roll of duct tape in his hands.

"Henderson, maybe you should use tape on those two. After you tape their hands behind them, tape up their mouths. We've heard too many rumors about them," Deke said.

Henderson pulled out a length of tape. "Do you really believe they took down an Apache?"

"Yes. I was watching when they did it. They planned and pulled off the whole little escapade in about five minutes."

Every time they had been captured before, Josh and Caleb had always figured out a way to escape. But this was beginning to look hopeless.

Maybe having an IQ of two hundred wasn't enough to defeat evil when it was as bad as these men. But God could, couldn't he?

Josh whispered a prayer then whispered to his brother. "Cabe, we gotta do something."

"I've got an idea," Caleb whispered back.

He looked up at the man approaching with what looked like a roll of Army duct tape. He replaced Josh's ties with the duct tape.

When the man turned to Caleb, he started rolling around on the cave floor and yelling. "You can't put that tape on me! I'm allergic to it and I don't have my inhaler!"

"Kid, your allergies are the least of my concerns."

"But if you put it on my mouth, I'll have an asthma attack and go into prophylactic shock. I won't be able to breathe!"

"It's anaphylactic shock. And if that will shut you up, start wheezing. It's fine with me."

"You mean it's fine with you to kill people?"

"You mean like **you** two did when you took down that Apache with two men onboard?"

Caleb didn't reply.

The look on Henderson's face told Josh he needed to say something. "Cabe, tell him. That Apache was going to kill us." Josh looked up at the man's lifeless-looking, creepy eyes. "Mister, wouldn't you kill somebody in self-defense?"

"Kid, you should never let it degenerate to a self-defense situation. You kill them before they even get a shot at you."

Josh studied the man for a couple of seconds. The evil showing in the man's eyes said he would kill without hesitation.

Josh looked at Caleb sitting beside him. "Ippa wona tap tap."

Caleb nodded. He'd gotten the message in the twins' language.

"What kind of nonsense is that?" The man pointed a long, boney finger at Josh.

"You made my brother so scared that he lost his mind and started jabbering," Caleb said.

"Shut up and be still." Henderson dropped the tape and put heavier zip-ties on Caleb's hands.

Caleb's conniption hadn't helped much, except to keep the duct tape off from his hands.

But now Josh had the duct tape to deal with.

Henderson went down the line, person by person, tying their hands behind them with heavier duty ties than the men had used when they had captured the six at the cabin.

So why were the twins going to get duct tape and the women were going to get heavy duty zip ties? The men must think tape is harder to escape from than zip ties. That thought spawned another.

Josh looked behind him at the lava rock embedded in the cave floor. Then glanced up at Henderson.

Henderson stopped when he came to Julia. "Deke, what about her?"

"Tie her ankles too," Deke said.

When Henderson turned toward Julia, Josh nudged Caleb and stuck out a finger pointing toward the rock that lay directly behind him, protruding from the gritty lava-dust-covered floor of the cave. The rock was jagged and it looked sharp.

Caleb nodded and whispered, "It might cut tape easier than zip ties. But then what?"

Josh shrugged. "I guess we do what Benjamin always says when he doesn't know what to do."

"You mean we wing it?"

Josh nodded. "Except it's not really winging it. God will show us what to do."

***

The scene before Deke dripped with sweet irony, as sweet as the sugary sap from a tapping spile driven into a maple tree. Julia Weiss, now Julia Bancroft, needed to understand this moment—what it meant for her and what it meant personally to Deke. This was justice for the murder of his brother. It would set the world right, as nearly as it could be after her crime against his family.

Deke pulled out a knife and locked its six-inch blade. He sliced the air with a quick motion, then took a step toward Julia.

Itzy tried to stand. "You can't hurt her. She's going to have a baby."

"A kid?" Deke said. "Great. Two for the price of one." He looked at Itzy in her shorts and pajama top and studied her for a moment. "But why should you care? Obviously, you're not **her** kid."

"Yes I am. They adopted me."

He let his leering eyes rove over Itzy's light brown face, medium-brown bare legs, and everything in between. He smirked. "In that case, you, my exotic beauty, I will save for last."

Chapter 22

7:00 a.m., McKenzie airfield

When Craig braked to a stop beside the McKenzie airfield, Daggett's Cessna sat fifty yards away on the edge of the runway.

Drew, riding shotgun beside Craig, pointed to their left. "There's Daggett looking at the tie-downs."

"Let's hope he doesn't intend to use them now. We need to be on that plane with parachutes strapped on." Craig backed the jeep until it was hidden in the trees.

The two got out and strode toward Daggett.

Craig stopped in front of the burly, grizzled old man who now stood beside his plane with one hand on the door. "What brought you back this way, Daggett?"

"Shoot. You can't keep secrets among the militia. I called another sentry and he'd heard what was going on out here. I figured out some of it myself. Any way I figured it, I thought you could use my help."

"You're right about that. Can you get us to the Skylight Cave?"

"This is beginning to sound like Deja vu—Steve Bancroft nine years ago."

"Our odds are better than his. We don't have two hundred Rangers to deal with, but we also don't have much time."

"So you two want to bail out over Skylight Cave?"

"If you've got chutes."

"Them I always have." Daggett pointed a thumb at the back seat of the Cessna. "Got four."

"How long until you can get us over the cave?"

"We'd better get the chutes on you before we take off, just to make sure everything's good to go. You can be on the ground in about thirty-five minutes, plus or minus a little."

"While you get the chutes, I need to call Baker and let him know what Drew and I are up to."

"Baker—that kid's a real dicer. A high-roller gambler. Just before we set down at Prineville, he let it slip that he'd never really flown a C-17. Had some time in a good simulator, but I was afraid he and the little lady would end up in a smokin' hole."

"Baker is game for just about anything. Maybe even taming that little lady enough to marry her, if we can get both of them through this day alive."

Craig hit Baker's number on his sat phone.

"Baker here. Is that you, Craig?"

"It's me. Wanted to let you know Daggett is picking up Drew and me at the McKenzie airstrip. We'll be bailing out over Skylight Cave in thirty-five minutes or so."

"Sir, I found a pilot at Kingsley who has a little time in a C-17. I'm—"

"I hope he has more time than you have. Daggett told me—"

"Colonel Craig, I now have over an hour in a C-17 including landing and taking off from austere runways."

"Austere is the operative word for you, Baker. So you're going to bail out of a C-17?"

"Sir, that's what the back end of a C-17 was made for, among other things."

"You're two-hundred miles away. How long will it take you to get to the cave?"

"We're taking off in less than five minutes and should be there in twenty-five minutes more. In about 30 minutes, maybe less, I'll be approaching the cave entrance."

"You'll probably beat us there, if your newly found pilot doesn't crash the C-17. Baker, if you hear someone behind you, please look before you shoot. And don't let anyone see you bail out."

"Not see me? That's not going to be easy. The C-17's loud. It'll attract attention."

"I'm sure you'll use your fertile imagination for an austere jump. But don't let them shoot you while you're coming down."

"That I can imagine."

"Baker, you do remember who's likely in that cave, don't you?"

"Yes. Shauna, by now, along with the six they captured, including Gemma and her two boys. We can't let anything happen to them ... to any of them."

***

Baker clung tightly to a hand hold as the big C-17 bounced to a syncopated rhythm while it ripped through the thermals at 8,000 feet above the Eastern Oregon desert.

Baker slipped into his chute and cinched it up. He donned his wireless, noise-cancelling headset and glanced at his pilot, Rex. "How far out are we?"

"We'll be over the target in about three minutes. You should start making your way to the rear."

"You got the coordinates of the cave, right?"

Rex glanced back at Baker and grinned. "You've only given them to me three times and double-checked them twice."

"But I need to bail out one hundred yards southeast of the cave. Momentum will carry me due south of it and I'll steer in a bit closer."

"If you want your jump to be precise, then it's important that you listen for my command. If you hear warnings through the intercom, like 'terrain, terrain, terrain', or 'obstacle ahead', just ignore them. That's Betty, the dreaded female warning voice, complaining about me flying so close to the ground."

"How close is that?"

"You don't want to be in the air one second longer than necessary. That's what you said, isn't it?"

"Right. I don't want them taking pot shots at me on the way down. But I don't want to become a human smoking hole either."

"Absolute minimum drop altitude is two-hundred fifty feet. So I'll drop you at three hundred. Don't wait too long to pop your chute, Baker. When we approach the drop location, I'll ask if you're ready. If you reply 'ready', then I'll give you a 'one, two, three, jump' command. Got it?"

"Yeah, I got it."

"Then you'd better get back there. I've got us shielded from the cave's location by Mount Washington, but we'll be visible from outside the cave for the last thirty seconds or so, and audible from the cave for about the same length of time. The rear will open as soon as you tell me you're in position. Good luck, Baker."

Baker hurried down the steps into the cargo area and strode toward the rear of the plane.

Lord, this had better work. I'm counting on you. So are seven other people. Please keep them safe from Walker's wolves.

"Are you ready, Baker?"

"Ready."

The rear of the colossal cargo carrier opened exposing Baker to a brown and gray terrain that rushed by at an incredible speed.

"One ... two ... three ... jump."

Baker leaped outward and plummeted toward the tree-dotted terrain below.

One thousand one, one thousand two.

He opened the shoot.

It jerked him to a stop.

The scene grew silent except for the fading rumble of the C-17's big Pratt and Whitney engines.

Baker spotted what looked like the location of the cave surrounded by tall pine trees—tall pine trees to which Baker was far too close.

Chapter 23

7:30 a.m., Skylight Cave

Josh's heart beat like a drum in his chest.

If he wanted to stop these three men from murdering all six of their captives, he had to get his hands free. And for Julia's sake, he needed to do that now.

While Deke's attention focused on Julia, Josh pushed the tape around his wrists against the piece of lava rock behind him. The jagged rock jutted up from the cave floor about six inches.

With the tape pressed firmly into the rock, Josh began a sawing motion, while he tried to keep most of his body still. It wasn't an easy thing to do, and soon the muscles in his arms cramped and throbbed, slowing his progress.

If Josh didn't hurry, the man with the big knife would stop his threatening and would use it on Julia. So far, he had only described what he would do with it and why. He hadn't hurt Julia, yet.

But if Josh couldn't put out of his mind some of those horrible descriptions of what the man wanted to do with his knife, he would soon throw up. That would draw attention to him and spoil his chances of freeing his hands.

Caleb's green face said he felt the same nausea.

When Josh studied Caleb's face a bit longer, he saw something else, something he had never seen on his brother's face before, hopelessness. It filled those haunted, pleading eyes.

That created an ache in Josh's gut that would only go away when Josh erased the hopelessness and replaced it by giving him something to hope in.

Usually, given a challenge, Josh relied on his own skills, knowledge, and intelligence. But this might take more of those three abilities than he had. Maybe it was time to do what Gemma did when she needed something—pray.

As he sawed still harder, he prayed.

Progress came slow, but the tape was shredding, just not as fast he needed it to or far enough to rip through it to free his hands.

A muscle in Josh's arm cramped hard from the contortions and stresses he had put it through. He tried to stifle his groan.

Deke lowered the knife and stepped back from Julia.

Josh stopped moving and held his breath. Had they heard him?

"Babak, Henderson, did you hear something just now?" Deke motioned with the knife toward the front of the cave.

"It sounded like a big jet somewhere in the vicinity," Babak said.

"That was a couple of minutes ago. I mean just now. It came from somewhere near the entrance to the cave."

While the men talked about what they had heard or hadn't heard, Caleb's fingers found Josh's hands and curled around them.

"Josh, I can feel the cut. You're halfway through the tape," Caleb whispered.

"I don't have enough time to do the other half."

Caleb's fingers seemed to have gripped the tape near the cut. "I'm going to try to rip it. Now, Josh." Caleb grimaced with the effort.

Josh pulled his hands apart with all his strength.

The tape gave. Then it ripped clear through.

When Josh looked up, the men's attention had returned to their six captives. But Deke was looking directly at Josh.

Had he seen them as they ripped the tape? Did he know what they had done, that Josh's hands were free?

Caleb straightened until he sat as he had before helping Josh.

After a few seconds, Deke turned toward Julia again. His twisted, evil grin said he was about to start using the knife.

Josh worked his hands free from the sticky tape but kept the strip of tape stuck to one wrist in case he needed to pretend to be bound.

Deke lowered the knife and again looked toward the cave's entrance. "I'm still hearing something." He paused. "Babak, I want you to guard the cave opening in case there is someone out there."

"I'd rather stay here and watch the fun when you—"

"I said watch the cave entrance. Get out there now!"

Babak swore, but he turned and strode toward the mouth of the Skylight Cave.

***

A few minutes ago, Shauna had hidden her car along McAllister Road and crept down the dusty trail to the Skylight Cave. But when she approached the entrance, loud and angry voices came from the cave.

If she understood correctly, a man named Babak would be watching the mouth of the cave. She wanted to hear what was happening in the cave. But for now, discretion was the better part of valor, if in fact Shauna had any of that quality.

She turned away from the cave opening and tried to move silently along the spine of the lava tube, headed westward.

Rough rocks and dirt bulged upward marking the cave below her. She wound around rocks trying to follow the cave.

A voice sounded a short distance ahead of her. It seemed to be coming out of the ground.

It came from a skylight. The hole was clearly visible in the sunlight.

But the morning sun in the eastern sky sent her shadow ahead of her.

Shauna froze when her shadow nearly reached the edge of the skylight. She would have turned the lights out in the cave, a deadly mistake.

Girl, what do you think you're doing? You just about gave yourself away.

The voice inside her head was right. She had nearly become captive number seven, or body number one.

Chalk up another failure to Shauna Jackson.

She had neither the time to debate that voice inside nor the evidence to make a case against it.

Shauna veered to her right until her shadow passed around the skylight. She then crept toward the hole in the ground from the west side, leaving her shadow behind her, opposite the opening.

After she passed a large boulder, the scene below came partially into view through the skylight. She craned her neck to—

The drone of a small airplane turned to a roar.

Shauna ducked quickly and crouched beside the large lava boulder.

The plane sounded close. Only a short distance to the east. But tall pine trees extending a hundred yards or more to the east blocked her view.

A plane in the area was a big concern. There weren't many small planes flying these days. It might have something to do with Deke.

With Deke here at the cave, Shauna couldn't afford to be discovered by some spy plane that supported him.

But Daggett flew today too. Would he—no. There was no reason for him to be here.

Shauna needed to keep hidden from any aircraft. And she needed a better look down that skylight where the voices had come from.

After the airplane sounds faded, Shauna approached the skylight. She crept on her hands and knees toward the opening, and she leaned forward to peer down to the cave floor.

The six captives sat along the cave wall. At least they were all still alive. Only Caleb and Josh were clearly visible because they sat in the edge of the column of light that penetrated at the sun's angle to the cave floor.

Two men in military fatigues stood in the semidarkness that surrounded the beam of sunlight. One stood directly under the skylight.

The twins' wide eyes seemed locked on the bigger of the two men.

One look at that man sent a jolt like a lightning bolt through her nervous system. Shauna recoiled at the awareness of evil. It oozed out of the man like something from a paranormal horror flick. That had to be Deke.

She leaned forward to get a better look at everyone in the scene below.

Her movement sent a trickle of dust and dirt particles down into the column of light, dimming it, turning it to a dirty shade of yellow.

Deke's head tilted upward.

Shauna pulled back out of view and stood, ready to run. But had he seen her?

She listened for any indication they might have spotted her.

"Did you see anything up there, Henderson?" Deke said.

"Nothing, sir," Henderson said. "See all that dirt and rock on the floor underneath that skylight. I'll bet those holes are constantly caving in, a little at a time. They get bigger, until the ceiling comes crashing down on—"

"Well, I don't plan to be here when that happens. It's time to finish our business and get out of this tomb. It's beginning to smell like death in here."

Shauna pictured Deke glaring at Julia when he said those threatening words.

She crouched and leaned toward the skylight, slowly bending at her waist, praying they were no longer looking upward, while she tried to peer in and see Julia.

Deke raised his rifle to the level of Julia's face and held it steady.

The impulse to shoot the man came from somewhere deep inside. But if Shauna shot Deke, would she be able to deal with the other two men after they knew she was here and had a gun?

She returned her focus to Julia.

Julia drew a deep breath and then looked upward, away from Deke and his gun. Julia's voice came pure and strong singing a melody vaguely familiar to Shauna—words about being ready to fly, ready to soar, leaving the world behind and asking God to open the door.

Tears flowed freely down Shauna's cheeks, but they suddenly stopped as another emotion filled her heart, rage. How could Deke just kill this innocent young woman who was expecting her first natural-born child? And he was going to do it while her adopted daughter watched?

Itzy's permanently tan face had turned pale, ashen.

The man called Henderson stood a few steps from Deke in a spot almost directly below the skylight.

Shauna whirled around and scanned the assortment of lava rocks near her.

She clamped her hands on a jagged one and lifted. It seemed to weigh twenty or twenty-five pounds. Shauna turned back toward the skylight and the scene below.

Julia continued to sing, and it seemed to have befuddled Deke. But he still held his rifle in the ready position.

"I will see my Savior's face and stand for all eternity in His amazing grace."

Someday, Julia, but not yet.

Shauna raised the rock above her head and brought it down with all the strength she could add to the force of gravity.

Her movement brought her shadow over the skylight, briefly darkening part of the light column shining into the cavern thirty feet below.

Henderson stepped to his left and looked upward.

With a clunk, followed by the cracking of bones and a scream, the rock drove Henderson's right shoulder into the stone floor of the cave, leaving him writhing on the ground with an arm that looked as if it had grown out of his rib cage. His shoulder was either broken, dislocated, or both.

Shauna stumbled and nearly slid into the skylight.

Deke's automatic swung upward.

To avoid falling into the skylight, Shauna leaped over it, tripped on a rock, and stumbled away from the hole.

The staccato cracking of Deke's weapon sent bullets ricocheting off the rocky walls of the skylight.

Shauna fell face down and covered her head as bullets screamed and whined after caroming off the sides of the skylight.

Chunks of rock must have been blasted off the skylight wall, because Deke's salvo was followed by the sound of rocks pelting the cave floor.

The clattering of rocks accompanied cries from Henderson. He must have caught the brunt of the falling rocks that would have added painful insult to his serious injury.

"One down, two to go," Shauna muttered softly. She had to think quickly because Julia would soon become Deke's target again.

Her tank top suddenly dug into her throat. Shauna gasped, coughed, and fought for a breath.

"Wrong. One down and none to go," the raspy voice above her said.

Babak. He was supposed to stay and guard the mouth of the cave. How had he—

"You make a lot of noise for such a little twerp. A lot of trouble too, especially if Henderson's moaning is your doing. Get up. It's time to add you to our collection."

Chapter 24

7:35 a.m., Skylight Cave

Shauna rose, whirled, and found herself staring down the barrel of a menacing weapon that she recognized. It was an M4.

So far, Babak had given no indication that he'd seen the Sig Sauer under her tank top, resting snugly against the small of her back. She would keep it that way as long as possible.

She looked up at the man behind the gun.

With a surly face pasted on a big, block-like head topped with a camouflage-colored cap, he was a sore sight for eyes.

His gaze was riveted to her face. "So you don't like what you see."

Before she could come up with any reply, cold steel banged into the side of her head.

She grunted and then tried to regain her bearings after seeing a flash of light from the blow.

"Be nice and quiet, girly. I want to see what's going on under that skylight." Babak nudged her forward while still gripping the neck of the tank top.

A foot from the elliptical hole, Babak jerked on her tank top, choking her again.

Shauna slammed a hand over her mouth to stop the cough building in her throat. She stopped near the skylight.

Babak stepped beside her and jammed the gun into her throat. "You be cooperative and quiet, and maybe I won't have to shoot you or throw you down the hole to visit Henderson."

What would he do after he saw how badly she had crippled his teammate with that rock?

***

Baker had waited too long to open his chute. He didn't hit the ground before his chute opened, but the momentum of the C-17 had carried his falling body too close to the stand of pine trees before the chute opened.

He pulled on the suspension lines, trying to swing his weight to the side of the chute opposite the big trees.

Too little too late.

The canopy hung in a fifty-foot-high pine leaving Baker dangling twenty-five feet above the ground and praying that the brownish-green canopy wasn't visible from the cave.

He worked his way out of the harness and climbed down the lower branches of the tree until he could drop to the ground.

He unslung his M4 and hid behind the tree trunk with the gun in ready position and listened.

No sounds but a dove cooing in the distance.

He crept through the trees until a lava outcropping appeared. It had a large hole in it that dropped into a lava tube. This was the opening to the cave.

Baker expected to see someone posted to guard the cave entrance so those inside couldn't be surprised. But no guard was visible.

Despite not seeing anyone, he approached the entrance cautiously, holding his M4 ready to fire.

He reached the ladder, which descended about fifteen feet to the cave floor, and stopped.

Voices came from farther back in the cave. The acoustics of the cavern seemed to amplify them, making it sound as if the people were standing beside him.

Baker listened.

"You would like me to shoot you, wouldn't you? You would prefer that to the knife."

"I would prefer that you just go away. But I suppose you will do whatever you want, Deke." Julia's voice.

Was Shauna in there? He couldn't see her. Where was she?

Regardless, Baker needed to break this up before Deke could carry out his vengeful intentions.

Baker slung his M4 over his shoulder and climbed down the ladder. When he reached the bottom rung, he looked farther into the cave. The cave ceiling dipped down at least ten feet cutting off most of the view of the interior. But beyond the dip, thirty or forty feet away, legs and feet appeared.

The brilliant beam angling down through the skylight created a surreal scene that made it difficult to distinguish the shadowy forms in its periphery.

Baker needed to move closer.

Deke's voice grew louder. He swore and voiced vulgar threats, mostly directed toward Julia but some toward Itzy. But the lack of evidence of Shauna's presence brought conflicting emotions, worry that she might have been caught and killed, and relief at the thought that she might not be here yet.

Baker crept closer until the entire scene near the skylight came into view. He saw Deke standing. Near Deke the dark form of a man lay on the cave floor. Along the cavern wall, six prisoners sat. But no Shauna.

"You leave Itzy alone or I'll—"

"Or you'll what, Ms. Bancroft? You know that I can't let any witnesses live. This is the end of the line for everyone here in this cave."

This had to be stopped now. "Freeze, Deke! Or it's the end of the line for you!" Baker aimed his gun at Deke's torso.

"Don't even try it, whoever you are, or Ms. Bancroft will be the first to die."

"Not if my bullet severs your cervical spine first at about C3 or C4. You won't be able to pull a trigger again, ever."

"I can kill Julia Bancroft before you can do anything. I have a magazine full of 147 grain hollow-point bullets."

The longer Baker waited, the more the danger grew for Julia. He stepped closer until he could see the entire cavern. "Put the gun down, Deke. Are you really going to gamble in a no-win situation?"

Baker flinched when a loud, gravelly voice came from above. "If you want to gamble Mr. Militiaman, let's up the stakes. I'll raise you by whatever this cute girl is worth, the one I found throwing rocks down on Deke and Henderson."

Baker looked up at the bright opening in the roof of the cave.

There were two silhouettes revealing a big brute of a man gripping the neck of a woman Shauna's size. The man pushed her head over the skylight.

The light shone at an angle that revealed part of the woman's face and upper body.

Shauna. And he had seen that expression on her face a few times. Anger. Anger that could get her killed if she didn't control herself.

Baker refocused on Deke.

Now the cave darkened with Shauna blocking much of the sun's beam.

Baker glanced up again at the skylight. "Munchkin?"

"Yeah. But this big baboon—"

"Munchkin." Babak's mirthless laugh that followed sounded like a barking dog.

"I've got an M4 and a Glock too. Are you gonna call us, militiaman, or are you gonna fold?"

Baker didn't reply.

"Say, Mr. Militiaman, have you got a thing for this tiny little—what was it you called her—Munchkin?" Babak barked another spate of laughter. "I'm raising my bid.

You've got ten seconds to put down your weapon, or I will blow Munchkin's head back to the Land of Oz."

***

Shauna needed to do something to stop this now. Baker's situation had grown impossible. One of the two men would kill him, and then Deke would proceed to kill all the captives in the cave.

Babak stood leaning over the skylight pushing Shauna so far toward it that she feared she might fall.

His grip on her loosened a bit.

This was her only chance to do the one thing she could think of to end Baker's dilemma.

Please, help me do this.

She grabbed the shoulder strap on Babak's body armor and jumped feet-first into the skylight.

Chapter 25

Baker heard a man's voice yell from above him.

The beam coming from the skylight went dark.

A loud thump truncated the man's yell.

Now Shauna's body plunged downward from the skylight tangled with the man's body. The big body separated from her and plunged down behind Shauna on her left.

Baker reacted instantaneously. He dropped his rifle and leaped under the skylight, arms outstretched.

He had to protect Shauna's head and still avoid the mammoth body that had followed her through the skylight. His powerful leap took Baker too far under Shauna.

Her body had rotated, becoming parallel with the ground.

Baker braced himself for the impact.

Gravity drove Shauna's one-hundred-ten pounds into Baker's chest. It took him to the floor of the cave.

His breath exploded from his mouth when his back hit the hard floor.

The muscles of his upper arm spasmed as they took the impact of Shauna's head.

The big man landed beside him in a face plant that made crunching sounds as the acceleration of gravity crushed him against the lava-rock floor. He lay with his neck at an unnatural angle.

Baker tried to take a breath. He croaked like a frog and little or no air came in.

He had experienced this before, and it would pass.

Whether the solar plexus is knocked crazy from the front side or the back side, the results were always the same. The big nerve ganglion couldn't pass along the breathe signal until all the nerve signals were under control, a process that might take a minute or so.

The back of Baker's head had a knot forming on it.

His head hadn't struck hard enough to see stars or to stun him. Maybe he had survived pretty much intact.

He tried to suck in another breath. Air came in but not nearly enough to fill his lungs.

Shauna lay on her back, stretched across Baker's upper torso. She sat up and turned to look into his eyes.

Their gazes locked.

Tears welled in her eyes then overflowed.

Shauna laid her head down against his cheek.

"How touching." Deke's voice.

How could Baker have forgotten the man bent on killing them? Probably bent on killing everyone still alive in this cavern. Maybe he'd hit his head harder than he thought.

Deke took a step toward Baker then backed away. Deke had picked up Baker's M4.

Baker's mistake was unavoidable. His choices had been either keep the gun or catch Shauna.

Shauna started to slide off Baker and get up.

"Slowly, little Miss Murderer. You have single handedly killed both of my team members without any weapon ... except that twenty-pound rock you dropped."

Henderson groaned. "No, she didn't kill me. Please, Deke. Just get me something to use for a sling."

"Henderson, I'm sparing you multiple surgeries and at least a year of grueling rehab, after which you might have some limited use of that arm that's sticking out of your ribs."

Deke's weapon swung toward Henderson.

"No, sir. I can—"

Three sharp cracks sent bullets into Henderson's head.

Shauna turned her head away to avoid looking at the cold-blooded murder of another human being.

"Baker," she whispered. "Siggie is still in my holster."

Shauna sat up on Baker's stomach. She faced Deke, shielding from his view the concealment holster under her tank top.

Deke pointed his gun in Julia's direction but looked at Baker. "I don't know what you two are cooking up, but I wouldn't try anything, or you'll be killing Julia Weiss."

"It's Julia Bancroft, you idiot. And you're the one who's a murderer." Julia spat the words at Deke.

"Okay, Ms. Bancroft. So the pot calls the kettle black. The fact remains that you murdered my brother, Captain Albert Deke. And you did it right here in this cave, where it's your turn to die. Justice being served here is the ultimate form of irony, don't you think?"

Baker's right hand slid under Shauna's tank top and across the warm, smooth skin of her back until it touched the cold steel of the hammer and the slide of the Sig Sauer. He pulled his hand toward his body until his fingers wrapped around the grip of the gun and slowly slipped it out of the holster.

Deke walked closer to Julia. He stopped near her and the twins who stood side-by-side along the cave wall.

Baker froze. Shauna would now be directly in Deke's line of fire if Baker used the gun and Deke was able to shoot back at him.

Shauna mouthed the words to him, "Do it now."

He shook his head.

Deke raised his M4, pointing it at Julia's face. "Any last words, Ms. Bancroft?"

Baker drew in a sharp breath. "Deke, I saw his military records and your brother was a jackwagon—a disgrace to the uniform."

Deke spun toward Baker and raised his carbine.

"Behind you, Deke!" Josh's shrill voice startled Baker. Josh stood like a pitcher throwing from the stretch.

Eyes wide and jaws clenched, Deke whirled back toward Julia.

With a strong throwing motion, Josh's arm whipped, and a large handful of gritty lava sand hit Deke square in the face.

Deke's hands went to his eyes. His bellowed agony echoed through the cave.

Baker couldn't risk hitting Josh or any of the others along the cave wall, so he aimed at the highest part of his target, Deke's head, and squeezed Siggie's trigger.

Deke dropped to the floor of the cave, nearly landing on Caleb.

Shauna jumped to her feet to help the captives.

Baker grabbed her arm. "Better let me check Deke first, Munchkin."

There was near silence in the cave as Baker approached Deke's motionless body.

No need to feel for a pulse. The damage to Deke's head told the story.

It was finally over.

"Deke's dead."

Josh, pocketknife in hand, sliced Caleb's ties and turned toward the others lining the wall.

Shauna headed for Julia, but Baker grabbed her arm.

"Munchkin, don't you ever do something like that again."

"Like what?"

"Like diving through a skylight."

"Baker, they were using *me* to kill you." Shauna's voice broke and she looked down at the gun in Baker's hand. "I—I had to do something." When she looked up at him, tear tracks streaked her brown cheeks.

Her words, her tears, the reality of what this selfless, young woman had just done hit Baker like a body blow from a professional boxer. It forced a blast of air from his mouth.

Baker sucked the air back in and pulled Shauna to him. He tucked her gun back into its holster, and he kissed her.

Despite the gruesome scene around them, Shauna didn't seem to object.

"Oh, yuck!" Caleb's voice.

"Double yuck!" Josh's voice.

Hands free now, Itzy, Kathy, and Gemma were clapping.

Shauna's big brown eyes gleamed in the column of light that beamed down on them.

Now her eyes went wide. She gasped.

Footsteps sounded near the mouth of the cave.

Baker grabbed Shauna's gun and pivoted toward the invaders.

Two large forms appeared, dimly silhouetted by the light leaking in from the cave entrance.

"You beat us here, Baker." Craig's voice.

"What were you celebrating?" Drew's gaze scanned the bodies on the cave floor. "Deke's demise?"

Craig chuckled. "You just couldn't stick to the curriculum, could you, Baker. And I've never seen winning a skirmish celebrated quite like that."

Baker drained his lungs in a long sigh. "That's because you didn't see what Munchkin did a few minutes ago. She took out two of these guys without even pulling her gun."

"That's a story I want to hear," Craig paused, "... as soon as you tell me that Deke has no more demons running loose."

"All the demons are in the bottomless pit," Shauna said.

Craig walked toward Henderson's body. "What happened to this guy's shoulder?"

"He got bombed with a boulder from the skylight," Gemma said.

Craig looked her way. "And the guy with the broken neck?"

"He snuck up on Munchkin and put a gun to her head," Baker said. "They were going to use her to force me to give up my gun so Deke could shoot Julia and then the rest of us."

Drew pointed at Babak's body. "Then how did he get down here."

"Munchkin hooked his body armor with her hand and dove through the skylight. The demon hit his head coming through, then he landed on it."

"I didn't dive, Runt," Shauna said. "I'm not stupid. I jumped."

"Oh, you **were** stupid. And you weren't coming feet first when I saw you."

"I was reclining gracefully so you could catch me."

"Reclining gracefully? Munchkin, you were flailing like somebody about to drown. You just happened to be more or less parallel to the ground when you landed on top of me."

"Drew raised his eyebrows. "And Deke didn't shoot anybody about that time?"

Baker nodded toward the twins. "Josh evidently got his hands loose and plastered Deke in the eyes with a handful of lava sand."

"You should have heard him," Caleb said. "Deke screamed like a little kid after Josh got him in the eyes."

"Like I said, Craig." Baker pulled Shauna to his side. "Munchkin took out two, and Josh set up Deke for his demise."

Craig's gaze swept the dead bodies on the cave floor. "I'll send a detail back to pick up these three. Now, I've got some news. First, Shauna hasn't heard about Governor Harper being kidnapped."

"Seriously?" Shauna said. "A brigade for the militia, kidnappers for the governor, and a revenge squad for Julia. Walker needs to go, now."

"I agree," Craig said. "The kidnappers may be headed our way. But about the JBLM troops—they appear to be pulling out. Steve's men with the JLTVs and close air support provided the knockout punch. Steve's providing a rear escort to ensure the remnants of the brigade go back to Prineville. We can't be sure, but it looks like the federal troops may be ending the battle for Oregon. If so, that might also end their support of Walker's unconstitutional attacks on U.S. citizens."

"Or they might just be planning a new attack," Drew said.

"Regardless, Baker, Drew, and I can fit in Julia's SUV, so we'll take it to help Steve rescue Governor Harper," Craig said. "We spotted Deke's van back in the trees. We can give it to Julia to take this group back to her house."

Shauna stared fiercely into Craig's steel blue eyes. "You mean, while I drive Julia's SUV to take you three to help Steve rescue the governor."

Baker gripped Shauna's shoulder. "How many times do you intend to put yourself in danger today, Munchkin?"

She looked up at him. "As many times as you do."

"So that's the way it's going to be?"

"If you want me around, Runt, that's the way it's going to be."

"We don't have time for this if we're going to get to Santiam Pass in time to help Steve," Craig said. "Shauna, do you promise to stay in the SUV and obey any other orders I might give you?" Now Craig's intense eyes burned into hers.

"Yes."

Baker stared at her for a moment, then shook his head. Shauna smiled at him.

He didn't return it.

Craig turned toward Julia who had huddled with the five who would go home with her. "Julia, check out Highway 126 before you get on it to make sure there are no federal troops in sight. After you pass through Sisters, turn onto Holmes Road and take the back roads to the ranch. That should keep you away from any residual action that might take place."

"Will do."

"Then let's go," Craig said. "I'm guessing we'll have to run down the kidnappers from behind. I want to reach them before Steve does."

Baker jogged beside Shauna as they double-timed it to the SUV. "You know, if you were a cat, after the events of this morning, you'd have about one life left."

She poked his shoulder, flashed her big brown eyes his way, and smiled. "One life. I think that's all I could stand to spend with you, Runt."

When they reached the SUV, Shauna climbed into the driver's seat.

Craig stopped beside the driver's door. "Don't you think our pilot should be driving us?"

"He hit his head. It almost knocked him out."

"Then I can drive," Craig said.

Shauna's hands gripped the wheel until the knuckles of her brown hands turned white. She wasn't budging.

"Give me one good reason why you should drive us."

"Hop in and I'll show you."

"I can give you one, Craig," Baker said. "We'll get there faster."

Shauna headed down the unpaved part of McCallister Road. "Sure wish we knew if where the kidnappers are."

"I've got an idea," Craig said. "Daggett is probably still at Roberts Field. I'll call him and enlist him to spot the van."

"So I need to head toward Sisters?"

"Yes," Craig said and placed the call.

"This is Daggett."

Craig had obviously turned on the speakerphone.

"This is Craig. Where are you and what are you up to?"

"You must want me to fly somewhere. I just refueled, so I'm ready to go. What's up?"

"We hope you will be, shortly. Daggett, there's a black van eastbound on Highway 20 somewhere around Santiam Pass. We need you to spot it without being obvious that you're looking for it, then call Steve. His JLTV radio can transmit on your frequency."

"What are you up to, Craig?"

"We're in Julia's SUV headed towards Sisters. We've got a little surprise planned for the guys in the van."

"Spotting the van should be easy," Daggett said. "I didn't see any vehicles on the highway until I was on the edge of Redmond. Climbing in now. Tell Steve to contact me in about five minutes."

"Will do."

"But, Craig, you'd better have a good plan for keeping the governor safe when you snatch her back. We need her alive. And maybe I'm plumb loco, but I'm gettin' to kinda' like that old battleaxe."

Chapter 26

8:15 a.m., somewhere along Highway 22

With her hands in nylon cuffs, an elastic fabric over her eyes, and a wide strip of tape over her mouth, Sandra Harper had few options for passing the time.

How long had she been in the big van? One hour? Two?

They must be going through mountains now. Sharp turns had slung her body side-to-side for the past five minutes.

There was only one person she could talk to, and it was someone she had a pressing need to talk to. But how could she begin a conversation with Him? How could she ask Him for anything when she was so undeserving of an audience with Him or of having her requests answered?

It had taken a murder attempt on her life by the President of the United States to get Sandra's attention. Since then, she had tried to mend her ways to do the right things, but would He even listen to someone who had lived a selfish, extravagant life, seeking power more than virtue?

Kate told her He was always listening, ready to hear. And her niece trusted Him with her life. Maybe that's what Sandra Harper needed to do, but first ...

Please, God, forgive this ignorant, selfish, middle-aged woman for all she's done. I've directly opposed your will and I may not have much time left, so I'm asking you to help me follow you like Kate does. You can have my life, for what it's worth, and I'll try to follow Jesus. Well, I will if you stop Walker's thugs from killing me before I even get the chance.

*Keep Kate, the militia warfighters, and their families
safe. Don't let Walker's troops prevail in the battle in
Eastern Oregon. And please don't let these goons use me as
a bargaining chip to endanger the militia. I'm placing my
requests in your hands because no one else can handle
them. So, in Jes—*

The tape ripped from her mouth, leaving her lips
stinging like they had been singed by fire.

Someone pulled away the elastic band covering her
eyes.

"I said, what are you up to, Madam Governor?" One of
Walker's goons jabbed her shoulder. It was the big guy with
burn scars covering half of his face. "If you're planning your
escape, don't bother."

She took a calming breath, trying to ease the pain
pulsating across her lips. "So my demise is imminent. In
that case, any extreme measures I take are warranted."

"Was that a threat you ..." He lapsed into a vile
description of her womanhood.

She tried to ignore both the profane outburst and the
urge to kick the man in his shin which was clearly visible
in the aisle of the van. "Do I look like a threat to you?"

He scanned her from her face down to her feet. "You
look like a well-preserved, almost attractive woman, a little
too ugly to sell to the traffickers. But I know a cartel leader
who would be delighted to keep you as a slave at his rancho
just to brag about how powerful he is, owning an American
governor."

"Did it occur to you that someone might consider me of
enough value to rescue me and kill you or this cartel leader
in the process?"

"You mean someone like President Walker?" The man
forced out a mirthless laugh. "No. He doesn't like you very
much. I think we shall sell you to a drug lord. One who will
make sure you lose your dignity, completely, and who then

will parade you around like a dog on a leash to demonstrate his power over Americans."

She scanned the view from the side window. Trees lining a mountain road and a lake.

It all went black when one of the men pulled the blinders over her eyes.

She had caught a glimpse of Detroit Lake on the right just before the blinders came down. "Where are you taking me?"

"To your new owner. To your grave. What does it matter? It's our choice, Governor, not yours." He turned toward the rear of the van. "Bring me the tape, Finley. I need some peace and quiet."

She fought the tape when they tried to cover her mouth. Maybe if they couldn't smooth it over her lips, it wouldn't burn so much the next time they pulled it off ... if that time ever came.

But it was clear that they were on Highway 22, headed toward Santiam Pass. Somewhere between the pass and Sisters, a battle would be fought. Maybe it already had been fought.

If only I knew the outcome of that battle, then maybe ...

"Listen up, men. I haven't heard from Colonel Blackford since we nabbed Harper. He should have overrun the militia by now, but we don't know his location or status, so keep it quiet in here while I make this call." The little beeps sounded like Scar Face was making a phone call.

"This is Martin, commander of the Salem Operation. Where is Colonel Blackford? ... That's not good. So what are we supposed to do with Harper? ... You didn't answer my question, sir. ... Extricate ourselves? Then who's going to pay us?"

Scar Face swore, finishing with some choice words for President Walker.

"Martin, what's going on?" It was the raspy voice of one of Scar Face's men.

"Stryker Brigade just got their derriere dropkicked. Colonel Blackford is wounded. Some grunt named Wright is in charge of a retreat back to Prineville. The battle's over. The militia whipped them all soundly and sent them to bed. Wright said Walker misled Stryker Brigade and advised we back out of any plans we made with him."

"We can't give Harper to Blackford as Walker directed. So who's going to pay us?"

"Dietrich, we have to pay ourselves," Scar Face said.

"What's that supposed to mean?" Dietrich asked.

"We do what I said when I was toying with Ms. Harper. We'll sell her to a drug lord who needs to boost his ego."

Dietrich cursed. "Why don't we sell her to Walker and ask for more money?"

"You idiot! We can't take Harper across the country and hand her off to Walker. It's too risky given the red areas we would have to cross. And Stryker Brigade is of no help either. After the spanking the militia and the air guard gave them, I think they bailed on the whole effort to help Walker. The status of JBLM in this little civil war is up in the air. I think the military is fragmenting just like the states. That casts a lot of doubt on us ever getting paid by Walker. Captain Wright said we need to come up with our own plan to extricate ourselves from the whole mess and then go home."

Dietrich cursed Walker and much of his ancestry. "The Commander-in-Chief can't command the military. He's in deep trouble."

"And that's why we head for the Arizona border, Nogales, where we meet with the CEO of the Cartel de Sinaloa."

"Martin, their headquarters is six hundred miles south of there."

"Yes, but their three vice presidents, all stay along the border."

"That gang of murderers would just kill us and take Harper, if they want her. At least call Walker, tell him what happened, and see what it would take for him to pay us." Dietrich paused. "The cartels are a mob of bloodthirsty savages. I'd like to keep my insides inside, if you know what I mean."

***

President Walker sat behind the Resolute Desk and watched Will Richards leaning back on one of the couches looking like he might fall asleep. That Will, his closest, most trusted advisor, could cast away all cares and take a nap in the Oval Office, no matter how much he needed it, irked Walker.

"Why do you suppose Colonel Blackford hasn't reported? Surely the fighting has ended by now."

Will sat up on the couch and rubbed his eyes. "Maybe the battle's not over. Or ... you know, the militia killed Blackford. Either way that leaves us in ..."

"I know where it leaves us." Walker reflected on the anger in his voice. He was beginning to lose it. That's one thing he could not allow to be seen, not even by his closest confidant.

Walker's secure sat phone rang. He looked at the caller ID. It was Tige Martin, the commander of the black ops team Walker had sent after Governor Harper.

Walker answered. "President Walker here."

"Mr. President, this is Martin, team leader."

"Please tell me that you have the governor."

"Sir, we have Governor Harper, but the situation out here is a bit sticky."

"I don't like **sticky**, Martin, whatever it means. Are you ready to turn the traitorous governor over to Colonel Blackford or not?"

"No, sir."

Walker swore for a few seconds then fought to bring his tattered emotions under control. "What's the status out there?"

"Mr. President, Colonel Blackford was seriously wounded in the battle. Stryker Brigade is in retreat back to Prineville."

Walker had almost exhausted his store of profanity. He wouldn't waste his breath using what little was left.

So Blackford and his brigade were bailing on him, failing to carry out presidential orders. That would get Blackford court-martialed.

But where did that leave Walker with a kidnapped state governor on his hands? She was a traitor. He could paint her as such and prosecute her. Or ...

"Martin, kill that spineless spinster. Just make sure no one can find the body any time soon."

"How much more do we get for a hit like that? It's a bigger risk."

"The same price I quoted you earlier."

"But, Mr. President, murder carries a much heavier sentence than kidnapping. It can be a capital offense. And if we run into anyone looking for the governor, we may have to kill more than just Harper."

"All right. You can have ten thousand more."

"Ten thousand more apiece?"

"No. Ten thousand more, period. You can pad your expenses a bit to make up for any inconvenience."

Walker ended the call before Martin could launch any more complaints.

When Walker looked over toward the couch, Will stared at him like he wanted to say something, but was reluctant.

"Whatever it is, out with it, Will."

Will shook his head slowly then met Walker's gaze. "It's all slipping out of your control, Wendell."

"What happened to Mr. President?"

"That's slipping away too. You're losing your military. Men are leaving their units and heading for a red or blue state where they can join up with a unit they trust. We have no Department of Defense, not one you can rely on. The one entity you **had** to control, the military, is out of control."

"I'm not giving in to anyone's demands. So what do you recommend, Will?"

"Plan C."

"Disappear? But that was supposed to be a last resort."

"Mr. President, if you wait one second too long, you won't even have that option." Will turned and left the room.

But Wendell Walker was not going to be the first president to go permanently AWOL. He would remain president, serve out his term, and somehow force this country back together ... even if it killed him.

Chapter 27

8:30 a.m., McAllister Road, near Skylight Cave

Shauna needed to reach Highway 20 before the van carrying kidnapped Governor Harper passed by them and escaped to the east.

She kept the mid-sized SUV about five miles-per-hour under insanity on the dirt portion of McAllister Road. But when she reached pavement on McAllister Road, she stomped on the gas pedal and broke the insanity barrier.

"Shauna, I haven't regretted letting you drive yet." Craig laid a hand on her shoulder. "But we can't help Sandra if we don't get there in one piece."

She didn't reply, but she did ease up on the accelerator.

"That's better," Craig said.

"What's that banging around in the back every time Munchkin takes a curve at double the posted speed?" Drew said.

Baker looked at the dashboard display. "The GPS says there's a half-mile straight stretch ahead of us. Why don't you unbuckle and take a look?"

"How much time do I have before the next turn?" Drew said. "Fifteen seconds?"

"Come on, Drew. Fifteen seconds for this straightway? That would be about 120 miles-per-hour. I'm not a maniac," Shauna said.

"Maybe not. I guess you just drive like one."

"Governor Harper's life is at stake. We can't let those thugs get by us."

Drew unbuckled, turned, and looked into the cargo area. "I see two boxes about eight- or nine-inches square. I think I can get them."

"Now you do only have about fifteen seconds," Shauna said.

"Got them. Good grief. They're heavy." Drew turned around, dropped the boxes in his lap, and buckled in.

The centrifugal force of the next turn threw him hard to his right.

The boxes flew off his lap and crashed into the door beside him.

Drew grabbed them again and ripped open the top of one box. "Weren't Julia and Steve going to put new decking in back near the children's play area?"

"I think they bought the materials to start the project but never found the time after Walker declared war on us," Shauna said.

"Well," Drew said, "we have two big boxes, one of wood screws and another of deck screws."

"Hang onto those, Drew," Craig said. "We might have a good use for them. I'm going to call Steve and finalize our plan to stop the kidnappers and rescue Governor Harper provided Steve's men haven't intercepted them yet."

"Don't dillydally, sir," Baker said. "I think we're getting close to Highway 20."

Craig tapped his sat phone and switched it to speaker.

Baker listened to it ringing.

"Bancroft here."

"Steve, this is Craig. What is your current location?"

"We're at milepost 94 on Highway 20, a little east of Black Butte Ranch. We're blocking all lanes of the highway and we're sweeping it headed westward."

"I take it that you haven't seen the kidnappers yet."

"No. But we're certain they couldn't have gotten past us. Reports from Salem say they're in a black van with five or six people in it."

"Is it safe to block all lanes while you're sweeping westward?" Craig asked. "What about civilian traffic?"

"It's safe. Because of the battle we anticipated out here, Zach has had all Central Oregon radio and TV stations tell people to stay off from Highways 20, 126, 242 and 22 west of Redmond. Residents of the Sisters area were told to stay at home and listen to radio or TV and be prepared to evacuate temporarily if ordered. In Western Oregon, they're warning residents not to drive Highways 20, 22, or 126 into the Cascade Mountains."

"Good. Then we should trap them between us, and there should be no civilians involved. Who and what did you bring with you?"

"We left two hundred men and a JLTV herding the brigade back to Prineville. But we repaired the other JLTV. I've got it and one hundred men in other vehicles. We can easily stop them. But, Craig, they could have more firepower than what you have in Julia's SUV. If they were to turn around and head back to the west, could you stop them?"

"We've got that covered, Steve. If they turn around, you just chase them until they run like their tail's on fire."

"Sounds like you've got a trap planned."

"I'm working on that. Call me back in about five minutes."

As Craig explained his plan to stop the kidnapper's van, his phone rang.

"Craig, Daggett has the black van in view," Steve said. "It's moving eastward across Santiam Summit as we speak."

"Then we've got ten or fifteen minutes before it reaches my position. Here's what we're going to do," Craig said.

"Julia's SUV has two big boxes of decking and large wood screws in the back. A thousand deck screws and nearly two thousand wood screws."

Steve chuckled. "Last time that amount got dumped on Highway 97, forty-five cars ended up stopped on the highway or in the ditch."

"That's the idea. We will deploy the screws at mile post 93. Can you line the highway with a hundred men, fifty men on each side of the road, starting about fifty yards east of the screws? String them out for two hundred yards down the road."

"I can do that and still keep fifty with me to rush them if they try to keep driving on flats."

"That sounds perfect. But make sure the JLTV is hidden, so they won't see it before hitting the screws."

"Right. That way we can move in quickly with a lot of firepower before they have time to react."

"Exactly," Craig said. "Pouncing on them as soon as they stop, or wreck, is the only way we can prevent a hostage situation. I just hope we don't cause an ugly accident and get the governor hurt."

"Me too," Steve said."

"I'm dropping off now to deploy the screws." Craig ended the call.

Craig pointed at the short sign along the roadway. "Here's our milepost. Drew, Baker, each of you take a box and dump them out of your window. Shauna, drive slowly down the center line of the road." He paused. "Is everyone ready?"

"Wait," Baker said. "Craig, tell Munchkin to stop."

"You heard him, Shauna."

After she stopped the SUV, Baker got out, opened the back end, and climbed in the cargo area. "I can cover the center and my side of the road from here. I was afraid if we tried to do that from a side window, we might accidently put some screws under our own back tires."

"Okay. Let's go, Shauna," Craig said. "Bombs away."

Screws clattered as they scattered across the highway while Shauna rolled down the center of the road at fifteen miles-per-hour.

"All done," Drew said.

"Me too," Baker said. "We just did our thirty seconds over Tokyo."

Shauna stopped to let Baker climb back into his seat. "I don't think Walker's men are going to see any humor in that. Let's just pray Steve's men can snatch Kate's aunt and then get out of there safely."

"The bend in the road, just before that screw garden we planted, should give the driver no time to react," Craig said.

A large vehicle rounded the turn a quarter of a mile ahead in the opposite lane.

Shauna stopped the SUV. "There's the militia."

Craig slid his window down and waved.

Someone riding on top of the JLTV returned his wave.

"Let's get this vehicle hidden, Shauna," Craig said.

"Munchkin," Baker pointed to their right. "There's an old logging road on the right."

"Take it, Shauna," Craig said.

As Shauna pulled the SUV behind a cluster of short fir trees, two lines of militia ran up the road on either side. The JLTV had disappeared almost two hundred yards down the highway.

"Windows down. Engine off. Now, we listen and wait."

"And pray for Governor Harper," Shauna said.

Chapter 28

Sandra Harper sat with her zip-tied hands folded in her lap. The blindfold had also obscured her view of time. Had it been four hours or ten since her captors captured her at Mahonia Hall? She wasn't sure.

One thing she was sure of, the road seemed straighter now, the curves more gradual. At least she wasn't bouncing between the door and the shoulder of the thug called Dietrich who sat beside her.

Another sharp curve pushed her against the door.

"What the—" the driver swore.

Something like gravel pelted the underside of the van.

The vehicle fishtailed in big, pendulum-like swings side to side.

The driver swore again. He seemed to be fighting the steering wheel.

"What's happening?" Dietrich's voice.

"Hit something. Flat tires."

The van leaned to the right, sending Sandra crashing into Dietrich.

Then it went beyond the tipping point.

Dear God, I do want to see Kate again. Please pro—

The van hit hard on its side.

She hung from her seat belt with the straps cutting into her right side.

Now the van slid along the pavement making an ear-splitting, scraping noise.

Dietrich screamed.

Sandra reached up with her zip-tied hands and yanked off her blindfold.

It took all her strength to shove her bound hands up to the window control. She hit the button and the window slid open.

The men in the van seemed occupied with staying alive and hadn't noticed her actions.

The van finally stopped sliding. It ended up in the middle of the highway.

Dietrich lay against a broken window with his hand caught between the window and the pavement.

The amount of blood around his trapped hand sent a wave of nausea through Sandra's stomach.

She put her feet on Dietrich's shoulder and pushed herself upward.

He didn't respond other than a guttural groan.

She reached her arms through the open window and put her elbows on either side of it. Sandra pulled her head up until she could look out.

A hand grasped her ankle.

She kicked.

Her shoe connected with something solid.

Someone below her grunted then swore. It sounded like the driver's voice.

Men's voices outside were yelling, but she couldn't make out the words.

She glanced at them and then pushed off from Dietrich again, raising half of her body through the window.

"She's getting away." It was a voice from the rear seat in the van.

A hand seized her ankle.

Incredibly strong hands gripped her beneath her arms, ripped her loose from the person in the van, and lifted her out.

For several seconds, the staccato cracks of automatic weapon fire drowned out every other sound.

Bullets pelted the van below her.

When Sandra looked up, she saw the face belonging to the man who carried her. It was a familiar face. Steve Bancroft.

Chapter 29

10:00 a.m., Black Butte Ranch, near Sisters

Shauna stood by Baker's side in the field near Black Butte Ranch. The militia had clustered here to plan the move of people and prisoners to various locations required to get them and their vehicles safely home.

Shauna watched Craig as he climbed up and stood on the JLTV. He towered above everyone and surveyed the group surrounding him. "Listen up, men ... and women! We have several tasks to complete before we can all go home. First, I just found out that all the troops from JBLM are at Prineville and are loading up to go back to their base. Congratulations to the militia involved and thank God for the CAS provided by the air guard that allowed us to defeat a larger, better equipped force."

Craig paused. "Here's how we're all going to get home and the tasks some of us will complete along the way. Drew West and I will escort the Governor to the Bancrofts' house at the ranch. Baker and Shauna will come with us so they can take one of our Chinooks from Madras and pick up the families from Kingsley. Half will be taken to McKenzie to drive vehicles home. Baker will go back to Kingsley and fly the rest to our rendezvous point at the Bancrofts' house, where we will debrief everyone.

"Steve, we need to assign two details to take care of a couple of things. One will take the two surviving kidnappers to the jail in Redmond. The other will transport the bodies of Colonel Deke's team from the Skylight Cave to Redmond for processing. If I had my way, I'd box them up and send them to 1600 Pennsylvania Avenue.

"On another note, I've received all's clear from all of our sentries in the area, so the rest of your men, Steve, can proceed to the ranch to be reunited with their families."

While Craig took questions from the men, Shauna pulled Baker away from the crowd around the JLTV. "I've only spoken a few words with Governor Harper, but have you noticed anything different about her?"

"Maybe," Baker said. He glanced at the governor standing with Steve by the JLTV. "She doesn't look traumatized by all that's happened to her. But this is the third or fourth time attempts have been made to kill or kidnap her. Maybe she's getting used to it."

"There's more to it than that. But changing the subject, you're going to have a long, lonely flight to Kingsley?" She studied Baker's expression.

He grinned. "Munchkin, I didn't invest all that training in you on how to load the cargo area of a Chinook just to let it all go to waste. We're going to have a full load of people, and I'll need someone to load them up and watch them while I'm in the pilot's seat. I don't want any civilians getting hurt on my watch."

"You know, Baker, that for two legs of this mission only you and I will be on that bird."

"So you finally stopped calling it a chopper."

"Don't change the subject. It's time that you and I had a talk, don't you think?"

"Maybe. What do you want to talk about?"

Shauna punched Baker's shoulder and regretted it when her fist felt as if she'd socked a rock.

"Hey, Jackson."

Great. Craig had approached them, and Shauna hadn't noticed.

"If you injure our pilot, I'll have you locked up with the kidnappers," Craig said.

"You need to arrest Baker for assaulting a woman."

"Munchkin, **you** punched **me**."

"You almost broke my wrist."

"How could I do that. I'm just a little runt that can't—"

"Is it safe to let you two fly a Chinook alone all the way to Kingsley? I can't afford to lose my pilot or that bird."

Craig hadn't included her in his list of valuables. Shauna glanced at him then looked away.

"Shauna Jackson," Craig said, "... after what you did today, I don't think anyone should ever underestimate you. Your courage saved six people and almost single handedly stopped Deke and his men."

"That she did," Baker said. "But why did you really come over here, Craig."

"I told Julia to expect a lot of company as people start arriving this afternoon."

"That will be an improvement over the company she had since early this morning," Baker said.

There was one detail Craig hadn't mentioned. What were they going to do with the C-17 that Baker told her he'd bailed out of at the cave? "Craig," Shauna said. "Our C-17 is down at Kingsley. Couldn't Baker and I just use a Chinook to fly some of our people to get their vehicles at McKenzie, while that C-17 pilot Baker found flies the rest of them up to Redmond? We could bring them back to the ranch from the airport?"

Baker shook his head. "No way. We can't do that. That guy at Kingsley's only got four or five hours of flight time in a C-17. Maybe six after he dropped me at the cave."

"That's more than you've had, Runt, and you flew all of us out of—what did you call it—an austere airfield?"

Craig chuckled. "She's got you there, Baker. But let's worry about the C-17 tomorrow. It'll be fine in Klamath Falls until we decide what to do with it."

"What to do with it? Sir, it's *my* bird. *I* got it and *I* flew it."

"You **stole** it," Shauna said.

"She's right," Craig said. "You can be sure it'll be reported as stolen by the folks at JBLM. That's a federal offense, Baker."

Craig plopped a hand on Baker's shoulder. "Once we get rid of Wendell Walker and put things back together in the nation and in the military, there will be a lot of messes to untangle. And there's still the issue of the ideological differences in these divided states. But we did make some progress today, if a costly defeat will make the federal troops leave us alone."

Shauna blew out a sigh. "But for the rest, we need to pray that Zach Tanner's message has a big impact on this broken nation."

Ten minutes later, everyone had their assignments and Shauna climbed into Julia's SUV. She sat in the back seat between Governor Harper and Baker.

Craig rode shotgun.

Drew West slid into the driver's seat then turned and looked back at Shauna and Baker. "I can't thank you two enough for keeping Beth and Peter safe today. That was a wild and woolly plan you hatched, Baker—stealing a C-17 and picking up our wives and kids at McKenzie. But you two pulled it off."

"I think they had a little help," Governor Harper said.

"You mean," Shauna pointed upward.

"Yes," the governor said. "And so did I."

Shauna made a mental note to tell Kate about this development.

To reach this point in her journey toward God, Governor Sandra Harper, alias Wicked Witch of the West, had come a long way in the past six short weeks. The question was, had she reached her final destination?

If was probably best to let Kate discuss that question with her aunt rather than Shauna inserting herself into a sensitive relationship issue between the two.

"You know, Shauna, I used to think you were a bad influence on Kate."

"Because of my Christian faith?"

"Yes."

"Just so you know, I thought you were a bad governor."

Sandra laughed. "I know. Sometimes I was. Sometimes I was a bad aunt. It wasn't intentional. But like Kate's mom, I really believed Kate was being foolish by joining those Christians at that church."

"But you changed your mind?"

"Yes, I did. When I saw the caliber of people she was associating with and even joining in a dangerous mission—Colonel Craig, Steve Bancroft, Drew West, Brock and KC Daniels—I decided not to judge her or her beliefs. So I joined that mission too. At first I did so more to save my skin than to try to save our state and our nation."

"Well, I'm glad you joined us. We couldn't have made it without your leadership, without the Oregon Guard, especially the Oregon Air Guard, and without your effort to flip the state from blue to red."

"And I wouldn't have survived without the militia."

"Craig says you're a natural born commander."

"I think he means I'm bossy."

Shauna's face stretched into a wide smile. "That too."

Though it was only 11:00 a.m., it grew quiet in the SUV. It had been a grueling, tension-filled time punctuated by violence and fears about not surviving. But somehow,

Shauna had survived. She thanked God for that just before she dozed off.

Something bumped Shauna's shoulder.

They were turning in at an airport. It looked like Roberts Field in Redmond.

Baker nudged her with his shoulder. "Wake up, Munchkin. This is where we left my Trackhawk this morning. We need it, because you and I have a long way to go before this day is over."

Chapter 30

11:00 a.m., Roberts Field, Redmond

Baker took Shauna's hand and pulled her gently from the SUV. Her other hand was busy rubbing her eyes.

She must be exhausted after the day she had—fired at three or four times, helped steal a military plane, severely injured one thug, risked her life to kill another thug, barely spared from being smashed on the rocks.

Baker glanced back at Craig in the SUV. "See you guys this afternoon."

"Come on, Munchkin. We need to be at Madras flight prepping our Chinook by 11:30. That's thirty minutes."

He unlocked his Trackhawk and opened the driver's door.

"What's the hurry." Shauna yawned. "Everyone's safe now." She slid into the passenger's seat and hit the recline button.

"Craig seemed to think something important was going down at 1700 today." Baker hit the ignition and the big engine rumbled its response.

"You mean the meeting and debriefing at the Bancrofts' house?"

He shook his head. "There's gotta be something more than that, but I'm not sure what it is."

The tires screeched on the pavement as Baker pulled onto the street. "Hang on, Munchkin. I've got some time to make up on our way to Madras."

***

Shauna glanced at the time in the Chinook. 11:45 a.m.. She and Baker were a little late, but they were in the big Chinook headed south toward Kingsley Air Force Base to start bringing the families home to the Crooked River Ranch area.

Baker told her that they should be landing at Kingsley by 12:45 p.m.. That gave them an intimate hour in the air.

They needed that time to come to some conclusions about **them**. But if she said, "Baker we've got to talk," he would clam up.

Maybe things would go more smoothly if she just started talking, drew him into the conversation, then steered it to the target.

Shauna studied Baker. With his hands on the controls of the big helicopter, he was clearly in his element. "I hope you don't mind that I forced myself on you today."

"You mean demanding that I take you with me to Prineville?"

"Yes. But I stuck to you like glue all day and you didn't complain too much."

"There was plenty to complain about, but it wouldn't have done any good, would it have?"

She shook her head. "We've spent a lot of time together over the past few weeks. How did that start? When did you first, uh ... notice me?"

"That's easy." Baker glanced her way. "When you started calling me irritating names after I landed on the heliport at the hospital in Salem."

"And it continued for most of that helicopter ride from Salem to the ranch."

"Yep. A cute, dark-haired girl with a sharp tongue challenged me."

"To what?"

"The taming of the shrew." Baker grinned.

"Not funny, Runt."

"See what I mean. She still needs some taming. But for a couple of years now, at least once a week I've had dreams about a cute, slender, dark-haired girl."

"Is that line supposed to impress me? Baker, you are full of it. How many other girls have you used it on? Besides, prophetic dreams were a rare thing even in Bible times."

"Prophetic? Munchkin, I didn't say it was *you* in those dreams."

"Well then who was it?"

He didn't reply.

"Runt, you are digging a deep hole for yourself."

"Okay. I didn't know it was you until I met you."

"There are women in our community who are actually beautiful. So why me?"

"Yeah. There's Kate and AJ. They look like twins. Then KC, the Celtic princess. They're beautiful but they're also married."

"What about Itzy and Kathy Gore?"

"Too young, but they'd catch any guy's eye."

"But the women you mentioned ... I'm not in their class, not when it comes to—

"Shauna, you are in another class—the most alluring, enticing, captivating class of all—one called pure cuteness." He paused and shook his head. "I'm not comfortable around beautiful and certainly not with drop-dead gorgeous."

"You mean like Susan?"

"Yeah. That's Craig's territory."

"To each his own." Shauna shot him a quick glance then stared out the side window at the mountains to the west.

***

It was silent on the comm system in the big bird for a full minute. Shauna had quit querying him. She just stopped with unspoken questions unanswered. How had that happened?

Shauna turned from the window and looked up at him again. "At least you know I'm not a proud person. I guess I'm a humble one."

I told you this subject wasn't exhausted, dude.

The voice inside his head was right. But now the subject needed to be exhausted ... exhaustively, whatever that took.

"Munchkin, humility isn't saying that you're deficient, not good enough, always coming up short. Humility is not thinking less of yourself. God made you, so you have infinite value. But humility *is* thinking about yourself less. And you demonstrated that today as much as any hero or heroine I've ever heard of."

"No. I didn't. I just did what anybody would do in that situation."

"No, sweetheart. Most people are paralyzed by fear in that situation, and they don't even think about actually leaping to their death to save others. Only the real heroes and heroines are willing to give their lives." He paused, realizing he had used the first real term of endearment that had ever passed between them. Munchkin, though he meant the moniker to be endearing, wasn't in the same category as sweetheart.

Shauna's eyes were welling. Now they were overflowing. "But I—"

"When you grabbed the demonic murderer's body armor and jumped through that skylight to drag him and you to your deaths to save all seven of our lives—I'd never seen that kind of unselfishness or courage. Not up close and personal. When I saw it, I had to save you. And somehow God used my feeble efforts to do that."

A muffled sob came from Shauna. Then the dam must have burst.

Baker had never seen her cry, not like this. What was going on in that sharp, baffling, female mind of hers? Had she finally seen the truth about herself? What a remarkable person she was?

Baker had to stop the crying before it broke his own heart. But helping a woman who was crying was like walking through a minefield. You never knew when you were going to tread on some buried detonator and an explosion would blow you away.

"Shauna, you don't bring bad things into people's lives. You tried to help seven people and nothing bad happened to any of them. Only good things happened. You saved their lives. And you were enough. You were **more** than enough. Any man I know would be proud to be associated with a woman like you."

Her crying stopped even more abruptly than it had started.

*Dude? **Association**? Is that the best you could do?*

Baker shifted his hands on the controls freeing up his right hand. He took Shauna's left hand and gently squeezed it.

She squeezed back. "Associated? What kind of association are you talking about?"

Maybe he had cleared the minefield without any casualties. Maybe the lights had come on in Shauna's usually sharp mind. But he had ended a good monologue with a boneheaded choice of words.

Better fix it, dude.

"Uh … a lifetime association. I'd be proud to have a woman like you by my side."

"A woman **like** me?" She removed her hand from his.

"Munchkin, it's **you** that I want by my side. You got me through this day—the most insane, treacherous, precarious day in my life. You latched onto me before I headed off to Prineville and you wouldn't let go."

Shauna looked up at him and smiled through her wet, welling eyes. "I guess not many women would endure gunfire and flashbang grenades to help you steal a cargo plane from the military just see if it could land and take off from McKenzie Airfield."

He laughed and felt part of the tension drain away. "We had a much more important objective than to prove the short runway capabilities of a C-17."

"I know, Baker. But insane is a good way to describe what we did. I can't believe we—"

"Neither can I. I guess it was desperation that drove us insane. Let's just pray that we're never that desperate again."

She reached across the console and laid a hand his shoulder. "You make it sound like we'll have more adventures together."

"I suppose we will."

His affirmation earned him only a demure smile.

Shauna forcefully blew out a sigh. "Do you think the war in Oregon is over?"

She had changed the subject, entirely.

Or had she?

Chapter 31

4:40 p.m., Crooked River Ranch

Shauna shoved out her palms toward the windshield as Julia's house rushed at her. "Baker, you don't have to land like you're going to crash."

"Sorry, Munchkin. But we're running late. We don't want to miss whatever's happening at five o'clock."

Baker had delivered the drivers to their cars in McKenzie. Most of those cars were now parked in the field across from the Bancroft mansion. Baker and Shauna had gone back for the others at Kingsley AFB and now were delivering the rest of the women and children to the gathering at the Bancrofts' house.

After Baker slowed their descent and touched down softly in the field by the parked cars, Shauna scanned the cars lining the circle driveway of the huge house.

One car had just arrived, Kate's car. And inside the house was Kate's aunt, Governor Harper.

If Sandra Harper was going to finish the story about the state of her faith, she would tell it to Kate, and Shauna wanted to be there to hear it.

She lowered the ramp on the rear of the Chinook and the passengers hurried down it to search for their vehicles parked in a line along one side of the big field.

Baker had shut the giant bird down and now he stood in the doorway to the cockpit. "Good job, crew chief."

"This crew chief needs to hear what the governor is going to tell her niece. See you later, Baker." She turned and ran down the ramp, then cut toward Julia's house, crossed the road, and followed Kate through the front door.

Once inside the house, Shauna tapped Kate's shoulder. "She's safe and well, Kate. I rode beside her from where Craig and Steve rescued her, at the scene of the car wreck, back to the ranch."

"Car wreck? She's had to endure so much."

"But she seems in good spirits, and I think she has some things to tell you."

"Thanks, Shauna. I think that's her voice coming from the kitchen." Kate turned and strode through the crowded great room into the kitchen.

Shauna followed Kate but remained several steps behind. She stopped after passing through the entryway to the kitchen and listened.

Kate scurried across the kitchen and wrapped her aunt in a warm hug. "I was so worried about you when Craig told me you'd been kidnapped. Then you were in a car accident. Are you okay, Aunt Sandy?"

"I think I'm more than okay."

Kate released her aunt and her frown lines deepened. "More than okay? What did they do to you?"

"The most important thing wasn't what they did to me, Kate. It was ... well, I made a decision, one that's been percolating for a while inside of me."

Kate's eyes widened and the twin frown lines disappeared. "Does this decision have something to do with my Christian faith?"

"No. But it has everything to do with *my* Christian faith."

The joy on Kate's face said it all. Her relationship with her aunt had been completely restored, only this time, it would last for eternity.

There were more tears and hugs than Shauna could keep track of, especially after her own vision blurred from unshed tears.

Were angels rejoicing right now? They had probably been rejoicing since late this morning. But Satan was cursing, just like President Walker would do if he heard of this ideological defection of Governor Sandra Harper.

If only this could be happening across this entire nation.

When Kate and Sandra walked into the great room, Shauna fell in behind them still a bit unsure about inserting herself into this moment between a niece and her aunt.

Brock stood under the big flatscreen TV having an animated conversation with Julia and Steve. "President Walker's an atheist, so he doesn't value human life. Let me give you an example of what I'm talking about." Brock paused.

Sandra tugged on Kate's arm to get her to stop near Brock.

He continued. "Well, as that famous atheist, Peter Atkins, said about human life, 'We shall have gone the journey of all purposeless stardust, driven unwittingly by chaos, gloriously but aimlessly evolved into sentience, born unchoosingly into the world, unwillingly taken from it, and inescapably returned to nothing. Such is life.'"

"Bummer!" Sandra blurted out.

Kate burst out laughing.

Brock gave Sandra a curious glance, then watched Kate laughing. "I guess irony is a form of humor."

Sandra sighed heavily. "I wasn't being sarcastic. Kate says that I should let you all know that I've joined your party ... politically and theologically. And she says that I'm now your sister because I'm a Jesus follower too."

KC, AJ, Beth, and Julia rushed to greet Sandra with warm hugs.

Brock squeezed through the huddle of huggers. "I'm glad that you, unlike our illustrious president, found the truth. People like Wendell Walker and Peter Atkins don't realize that science can't provide the answers you dubbed 'bummer' without exposing its inability to transcend the domain of science in order to make implications about beginnings and to comment on meaning. Fortunately, there is a worldview that doesn't suffer from the limitations of science or the errors of Scientism, one which provides intellectually satisfying answers to the human condition. The biblical worldview. I'm glad you found it, Sister Harper. And I'm glad that you found the one who gave that worldview to us and illustrated it through his life, Jesus."

"That was a mouthful," Beth said.

KC laughed. "And a headful."

Sandra smiled and shook Brock's hand. "I'm glad too, Brother Daniels." She paused. "It's not like I've never delved into your metaphysical world, Brock. I've studied enough to know that science cannot transcend its domain. And when some scientists try that, well, they're just being a chip off the old crock."

"Good one." Brock laughed and it quickly spread, drawing those from the other side of the great room to see what the commotion was all about.

Sandra's eyes sparkled with delight. She was finally home among people with whom she belonged.

"For Kate and for Sandra, thank you, Jesus," Shauna whispered.

"Me too." Baker had crept up behind her.

"So you heard?"

"Munchkin, she all but told us as much while we rode home in Julia's SUV."

"That's what I was thinking too."

"Listen, everybody!" Steve's voice. "It's almost five o'clock. Zach's broadcast is being streamed live and tonight there will be live callers from across the nation. The local station is broadcasting his program, so we're tuning it in and playing it through our sound system. If your kids don't want to listen, Itzy and Sam will watch them in the back yard."

The room grew quiet and soon the fanfare for Zach's show played through the powerful speakers, filling the great room with the power of epic orchestral music.

Chapter 32

5:00 p.m.

"Welcome to Zach's Facts on the Restore America Network. We have a lot to cover tonight, so let's go straight to my monologue.

"Today, President Walker, in violation of the Constitution, ordered military troops to attack the Central Oregon Militia and tried to attack the militia leaders' families, including their children.

"In addition to that, he sent two teams of special forces in black operations to kill the wives, children, and friends of three militia leaders' families and to kidnap the Governor of Oregon, Sandra Harper.

"I am glad to report the troops were routed by a smaller force of militia and both black operations ended with the perpetrators either being killed or taken into custody.

"Wendell Walker is a failure as a leader of America and a failure when he tries to destroy it.

"As you can see, President Walker's feigned emotional appeal to Americans for unity on the first day of his presidency was simply a diversion. Since then, he has tried heavy-handed tactics to force us to conform to un-American policies, policies that rob us of our freedoms and threaten to tilt America to the radical left in proportions that are historic.

"He has attempted to wipe out all vestiges of the America we have known and loved, and to teach us to accept the control, surveillance, and subservient lifestyles required for good little citizens of a global, socialist government.

'Over the last two months, his heavy-handed tactics have included covert and overt military action against American citizens, including the attempted assassination of a governor. He has also used martial law to control a populace that no longer wishes to obey his unconstitutional demands. This has driven our nation to an informal secession, where most states are taking measures to protect themselves from the federal government run by the tyrant, Wendell Walker.

"Seeing his attempts to control states flounder—states like Oregon, which he evidently meant to use as an example of what happens to those who step out of line—Walker has tried to order military units to attack civilians. I have already reported to you President Walker's attempted invasion of Oregon and its complete failure.

"Honestly, I do not know if any significant part of our military will take further orders from this president who has no qualms about issuing unconstitutional orders. If that is truly the case, then Walker is on his way out, one way or another.

"Regardless, the shape of American politics for years to come has been cast in the concrete of diametrically opposed worldviews, deeply held convictions which are incompatible. These opposing beliefs on morality, ethics, the nature and value of human life, the source of authority, and thus on the interpretation of the Constitution, have split the nation roughly fifty-fifty since the '90s. As an American, I'm afraid you'll have to learn to live with this ideological civil war.

"But there is one way our nation can come together, united, and ready to govern itself once again. That way is to follow the path we walked nearly three hundred years ago, beginning in 1726. God moved mightily across our nation, calling men and women to repentance. This movement of His Spirit, the Great Awakening, prepared us for what happened in 1776, when we declared the United States to be a self-governing nation, ready to take its place among the nations of the world.

"Many of those who follow my broadcasts have been praying for such a movement, another awakening that turns our nation back to the ultimate source of authority, God.

"The defeat of President Walker's forces today opens a door for us, but in order to walk through it, we need to recover from the ungodly, immoral, and insane policies and leftist dogma that has been crammed down our throats. We have married Molech by sacrificing millions of our unborn children to our selfish desires. We have ignored God's record of our creation. We were created in His image, male and female. We have perverted that image, manifested in two genders, and have instead said that man defines his own gender whenever he wants to, based upon his sexual appetite for the day.

"We have redefined the purpose and nature of work. The Bible says that every man should eat and drink and enjoy the good of all his labor—it is the gift of God. It goes on to say that if anyone is unwilling to work, he shall not eat. Notice it doesn't say 'he who can't work', but God made it an issue of the will, 'he who won't work' shall not eat."

"The list of inconsistencies and contradictions of Walker's way with the American way goes on and on.

"Rather than Leftists in America struggling to justify all their political positions, it is easier for them to vilify those who won't accept their politics, as President Walker has done.

"But we have now reached a critical moment in time where the nation must humble itself and repent, turn from its evil ways, and pray that God will heal our land, that we might once again become one nation under God. Unless we do this, I see only centuries of darkness ahead. Not just for America, but for the entire world should Marxists gain control.

"Daniel Webster was right when he said, '... if the American Constitution should fail, there will be anarchy throughout the world'."

"I will be back after a commercial break and we will, for the first time, take live calls from our listening audience. My assistant, Tim Calhoun, will answer your call and pass you on to me. Our number is 541-447-6770.

"We're back, folks, and Tim says we have a call from someone that we all need to hear from. It's a member of Calvary Church in Knoxville, Tennessee. Put him on, Tim.

"This is Zach Tanner. With whom do I have the pleasure of talking with?"

"My name is Milt Demeritt. Thanks for taking my call, Mr. Tanner—"

"I'm just Zach, if you don't mind."

"Okay, Zach. We're seeing something here in Knoxville that only the Lord could do."

"Please share it with our radio audience."

"Well, it started a couple of weeks ago in the early Sunday morning prayer meeting, where a few of us gather to pray for the Sunday services and other requests people bring to us. We had fifteen people total, including four new people. Two weren't even church members. They said they weren't even committed Jesus followers, but they were looking for something solid to hang on to in these tumultuous times.

"All four committed their lives to Christ that morning. So did five or six people in the Sunday service. After the service, our prayer group met again, only we had grown from fifteen to fifty.

"Prayer didn't stop at the end of the day, but it has continued nonstop for almost two weeks. We've been praying for our nation, for people to repent and turn to Christ, and for people to wake up before it's too late for America.

"This has been going twenty-four-seven, and now we have three to four hundred people praying around the clock. Two other churches in the city have joined us.

"I read that book, 1726 by Dr. Hyatt. This sounds like what happened then, and it happened again before the Civil War."

Baker tapped Shauna's shoulder. "Munchkin, you really laid into Zach about this and now look what's happening."

Had God used her for something this far reaching? Probably not.

Baker read the doubt in her eyes. "He did, Shauna Jackson. He used you."

"1726. Let's pray that's true," Zach said. "Milt, thanks so much for sharing that encouraging news."

"Well, you heard the facts folks," Zach said. "God is moving in Knoxville Tennessee. Hearts are turning to the Lord. Concern for the nation is growing and prayer is going up from at least one of the nation's cities."

"What's that, Tim? ... We have another similar call? ... Okay. Put her on."

A young woman from Lancaster Chapel in Pennsylvania told a story almost identical to the man from Knoxville.

"This is incredible," Zach said. "Do we have any more callers, Tim?"

"We sure do. I have twenty callers on hold, all with similar stories. They are all saying that they haven't been able to get their story out beyond their local areas because of the president's opposition and due to the fragmentation of the states. Our holding queue is full, and some folks are undoubtedly getting a busy signal. What do you want to do, Zach?"

Kate's voice rose above the buzz in the great room. "Keep going, Zach! Talk to all of them. America needs to know what's happening. God isn't finished with this nation yet."

The buzz in the great room rose to a rumble, urging Zach to keep going. Of course, he couldn't hear, but Shauna Jackson could. She looked up into Baker's beaming face.

"Don't let anyone tell you that you are small and insignificant, Shauna Jackson. I've seen you deal with life-threatening danger, sacrifice your life for others, use your genius to stop an evil man, and to cap it off, you've influenced Zach Tanner to initiate and announce a movement of God across this entire nation."

She leaned against Baker and curled a hand around his waist. Words for a reply didn't come. Only tears, but they were tears of joy.

Yes, keep going, Zach. God isn't finished with America yet.

Chapter 33

Sandra Harper slipped into a quieter corner of the great room as the events of the day streamed through her mind like an intense thriller movie. What a day it had been, and this was only day one of her trust and commitment to God.

What did her future hold as she walked through life with her Heavenly Father? It certainly would not be the boring, misguided, intellect-dulling sort of life she had pictured Christianity as being. The God of the universe wasn't anything like that. He moved in the hearts of people. He encouraged and empowered them to perform exploits that would be impossible for people who didn't know Him.

Words she had heard as a little girl, omnipotent, sovereign, took on vivid meanings after what she had witnessed throughout the day, a day ending in what looked like the beginning of a restoration of this nation to its godly roots.

Sandra had always attributed the nation's founding to the strong desire for freedom and perhaps a bit to the morality of the religious people among the founders. But to God's sovereign plan for this nation—she had scoffed at people who expressed such a notion.

On the radio, Zach was still taking callers. Each one told a similar story, and with each story, the energy in the room grew as the stories resonated in the hearts of these warriors, their wives, and their children.

The twins, Josh and Caleb, were using one corner of the room to put on a play for the younger kids. It appeared they were acting out, in a melodramatic fashion, the Skylight Cave rescue.

While Sandra watched, Kate had slipped in beside her. That was Kate's husband to be on the radio. Zach would have the most beautiful bride in Oregon.

"Aunt Sandy, who's going to tell her, you or me?"

"You mean Laura?"

Kate nodded. "My mother with whom I'm not on speaking terms."

"Maybe that's a good reason for **you** to tell her."

"I've tried. But she doesn't respect me, my beliefs, or anything I have to say."

"I wouldn't know what to say, Kate. I'm brand new at this."

Kate took her hands. "Just tell her your story. How God reached out to you and showed you how much you needed him."

"Well, the truth is President Walker had a lot to do with that."

"Then tell my mother how an evil president made you feel and how that convinced you that only a good God could stop the evil and meet your deepest needs."

"If you look at it that way, I guess I can do that."

"Just a second. I'm getting a call. It's from Zach. The show's still on the air, so this must be important."

"How's it going, sweetheart? ... So you're finally getting a break. God reclaiming America. It's a real game-changer. ... What? She can't do that. Aunt Sandy's standing here beside me. ... I'd better go, Zach. I've got to tell her now. ... See you later. Bye."

Obviously, Zach's message affected Sandra in some way. "So what's so important about me standing beside you?"

Kate blew out a blast of air. "Zach heard some news at the radio station. Secretary of State, Layla Thomas, is saying that, after the kidnapping, Governor Harper is either dead or unable to serve and Thomas is trying to get sworn in as governor."

"***That slimy little snake!*** Kate, I need to borrow your phone. My official phone never turned up after the abduction."

"Here's my phone. I'm going to tell Craig about this while you make your calls."

There were only a few numbers that Sandra had memorized for emergencies. The rest were in her contacts list.

One number she memorized was the emergency phone for the Oregon Chief Justice, Jacob Finley. Another was the person in charge of her security.

She keyed in Justice Finley's number. He answered on the third ring. Thank heaven she wouldn't have to deal with voice mail and wait for a return call.

"Justice Finley, this is Governor Harper. What's this nonsense I hear about Layla Thomas trying to get sworn in as governor?"

"It's good to hear your voice, Governor. Ms. Thomas says that she hasn't heard from you and can't get any response from your cell. After hearing of the kidnapping, she said that something must have happened to you and—"

"Yes, a lot happened to me, but I'm fine. I was rescued by the militia this morning somewhere near Sisters. I was waiting for my secure cell to turn up, but it didn't, so I haven't called State Police Special Operations Commander yet. Will you please let Major Sellers know that I'm unharmed and spending tonight at the militia ... uh, headquarters near Redmond. I'll make arrangements to return to Salem tomorrow."

"What do you want me to tell Layla Thomas? She's sure to inquire as quickly as she's moving."

"Tell her that usurping my authority is in violation of the state's constitution. Am I correct, Jacob?"

"Basically, that's correct. Although, being unsure about your status might make that judgment less than straightforward."

"Also tell her to be glad that she's elected and not appointed like most of the others on my staff, or I would fire her immediately. Instead, I think I'll arrest her. Call me at this number if anything important comes up. Otherwise, I'll see you tomorrow."

Sandra ended the call.

Craig walked her way. "Did you tell everyone you're alive and kicking, especially the slimy little snake?"

"Did you hear that part?"

Craig laughed. "I'm pretty sure everyone in the room heard it."

"Layla Thomas wanted to be sworn in as governor due to my circumstances."

"I take it she won't be."

"That's right, Craig."

"Well, we're bringing in a bunch of folding chairs that Julia and Steve keep in their garage. Grab one. I'm about to call our militia meeting to order."

***

At 6:30 p.m., David Craig stood in front of the large, flat screen TV at the head of the great room.

"Sam and Itzy are taking the kids to the back yard where I'm sure the twins will continue their Oscar-winning production of the Skylight Cave drama. So our meeting is called to order." He paused until everyone settled into a chair or found the spot where they would stand.

"God seems to be moving across this nation in ways we haven't seen since the Jesus Movement, maybe not since the Great Awakening of 1726. And we may have won the battle with President Walker. Be that as it may, we still need to be vigilant.

"As best we can determine, our series of resounding defeats of Walker's forces has left him with no troops in the region who will follow his commands. That's why he sent that team of misfits via a black operation. But Walker didn't realize Colonel Deke, the leader of that group of thugs, was bent more on revenge for his brother's death than on carrying out the president's orders.

"Events like what happened at Skylight Cave are the kind of threats we need to be prepared for from Walker in the future. I will lead a team of selected warfighters to plan for these contingencies."

He made eye contact with Beth West. "I will need a report on our available funds from you, Beth. Then you, Drew, Steve, and I need to form a plan for using those funds to restock the militia so we don't run short of critical supplies.

"The best way to ensure we don't have to fight again is to look too strong for anyone to challenge us. We'll need munitions, better gear, including better helmets and body armor. I'll be negotiating alliances with other likeminded states and geopolitical areas to make attacking us, or any of our allies, extremely unattractive to Walker and to any still loyal to him. This will also deter any enemies of the United States from thinking they can establish a base of operations in our area."

Baker raised his hand.

"What's on your mind, Baker?"

"Sir, don't forget we've got several Chinooks and a C-17."

"Yes, we've got them," Craig said. "But can we afford to fly them?"

"I'll need your fuel requirements," Beth said.

Baker rubbed his chin for a moment.

"I don't have to have the information tonight," Beth said.

"But you need a rough idea, because when you hear how thirsty that big bird is—well, the C-17 burns about 2,000 gallons per hour in normal flight operations. Jet fuel is at almost five dollars per gallon. A rough estimate is $10,000 per hour for the C-17. I recommend we keep it fueled up for a five-hour flight, just in case."

"That's fifty thousand dollars," Beth said.

"I can help with part of that expense," Sandra said.

"You'd better put in the Chinooks too," Craig said.

"They're cheap." Baker grinned. "Only about fifteen hundred dollars per hour."

"Put in another fifty thousand for the Chinooks," Craig said.

"Done," Beth said. "So far we've spent a hundred grand on gas."

"Please, spare me the details until you've had time to put together a complete report," Craig said. "If you've got any new ideas for raising funds, put them in the report too, Beth."

Drew slung an arm around Beth's shoulders. "But you can't sell our horses."

She tweaked his nose. "You know I would never do that."

"Moving right along," Craig said. "Tomorrow, Company A should take the day off to get your families settled in at home while Company B is on duty. The next day Company A will be on duty while Company B gets their houses in order. By then we should have our plan for restocking, repairing, and such to prepare for any further conflict."

"Susan, do we have any new intelligence that might give us a clue what to expect in the near term?"

"While we were down at Kingsley, I talked to their intelligence officer. He noted that the military's intelligence communication network was not designed for a fragmented military that was fighting against itself. So we're getting intelligence that wasn't intended for the Guard at Kingsley or Portland. Eventually, they might cut off the intelligence broadcasts so that we don't get them. But the word spreading throughout the intelligence network is that the military is reluctant to undertake any operations ordered by President Walker against American civilians or military."

Susan paused. "I guess that means the fighting should settle down while the political issues are being worked out. But who knows where we'll be when the political dust settles? And on the civilian side, you all heard Zach's broadcast. It looks like the majority of the people could unite sooner than we thought. Although, the radical left will never unite with us."

"But hopefully, they end up being a small minority that no one is willing to listen to again, ever. Any other concerns we need to discuss tonight?" Craig stopped and looked around the room.

No hands and no voices. "Okay. Then would someone like to close for us in prayer."

"I will."

Craig's gaze focused on the person whose voice he recognized. He smiled. It was a brave but well-conceived move for a baby Christian seeking to bond with her fellow believers.

"By all means, Governor. Close this meeting for us."

Her prayer was simple, heartfelt and to the point. She didn't miss any of the main points regarding issues facing the people of Oregon or of the United States.

Sandra Harper hadn't a clue what a gift she was to Oregon or how much God was using her to heal a broken land.

Eight weeks ago, she was a rising star in Walker's socialist organization. Now, she was Craig's strongest ally and a woman God was using to unite and protect a free America.

Craig peeked midway through the prayer. Across the room, standing by her aunt, Kate Alexander was grinning from ear to ear.

Sandra's prayer ended with a hearty amen from the militia members.

As some parents headed for the backyard to claim their kids, Susan worked her way through the people to Craig's side.

"Wasn't it a great meeting, David?"

"It surely was. I'm hoping that, after the dust settles, we'll be ready for the next general election coming up in about sixteen months."

Susan turned to face him. "I guess that leaves us with mostly some local issues to resolve."

"Didn't you and I cover those already?"

"No. We only covered the military issues. Sweetheart, there are at least two weddings that have been placed on hold while we dealt with Walker, and now Walker's finished.

"*At least* two weddings? Kate and Zach have changed their date twice already and we haven't even set one."

"Exactly." Susan grabbed his gaze with hers and wouldn't let go.

"But you said 'at least'. Is there another lucky couple?"

Kate approached them. "So, our leader wants to know who the other lucky couple is. Any thinking person would know that after what Shauna and Baker have gone through together in the past forty-eight hours, no one will be able to pry those two apart."

"But they aren't even engaged yet."

"David, after all that time they were together, you could be wrong about that. And you just changed the subject. What about *our* wedding date?"

***

The big clock on the great room wall said it was a little after eight o'clock when Baker led Shauna into the kitchen, out the back door, and he didn't stop until they reached the edge of the bluff.

From this location, perched on the edge of the escarpment, they could see the ranch golf course to the east. The sun, near the Cascade peaks to the northwest, sent long shadows from juniper and pine trees streaking across the brilliant green grass of the golf course. The yellow cast created by the rapidly sinking sun produced a picture that looked more like a master artist's painting than a real-world scene.

This would do wonderfully for what Baker had planned.

Shauna's gaze scanned the plateau below. "Wow. I could never tire of this view."

"And I could never tire of having you with me, no matter where we are."

Shauna met his gaze. Her eyes widened and she sucked in a short breath.

"Shauna Jackson—"

"Stop. Baker, if you want to ask me something, you need to speak to me like you normally do."

"Okay." He took both of her hands but didn't kneel like a beggar. He stood like a man looking at his equal. "Munchkin, at the first chance we get, will you marry me?"

Shauna's mouth opened to speak, but no words came out. Was that a no, a hesitancy, or something else?"

"Munchkin, you don't have to give me your answer right now. We both know that mixed marriages have more challenges to overcome and—"

"Baker, every marriage is a mixed marriage—two different people raised in two different families often in different parts of the country. It's always a challenge, especially if people aren't committed to God and to His institution of marriage **before** they commit to each other."

"I'm committed."

"And I ought to be committed for agreeing to marry a runt like you."

"So your answer is yes?"

"After we work out some details, it *will* be yes."

"You won't regret this, Munchkin. You'll see." He reached for her.

"Take it easy. I'm not going anywhere." She paused. "First the details. Where are we going to live?"

"I've got a motorhome, but we can't live there."

"Why not?"

"You deserve something better than a bachelor pad. Besides, it's too small."

"I think Zach and Kate plan to live in his motorhome until they find something else."

"Shauna, Kate owns Crooked River Espresso, and she comes from a wealthy family. They can find something else faster than you can bat those long eyelashes of yours."

"All right. Where do you propose we live?"

"If we sell my motorhome, we can use the money to buy a lot and building materials to build our dream house here on the ranch."

"How fast can you build?"

"Some of the militia troops will help. It might take a few months, but—"

"Baker, it will take time to find and buy the lot and time to build the house. What are we going to live in while that dream house is being built? We're sure not going to live in one of Julia's bedrooms after we're married."

"You're right. That wouldn't be, uh—"

"I think you need to schedule a counseling session with Beth. She has an MBA and can probably give you some better suggestions, like ... you borrow the money to build the house using your RV for collateral and then build our house. You can sell your motorhome and pay the loan after we move in."

"Guess I don't need a session with Beth. Did I answer all your questions?"

"No. You're just trying to **nail down** my yes before your answers are so bad that I revoke it."

"Up until today you've liked my answers. Why are you interrogating—"

"As a husband you are supposed to provide for your family. What's Radley Baker going to do?"

"I'm a pilot, Shauna. I'm going to fly."

"What will you fly? And who will you fly it for?"

"I'll fly anything my employer wants me to fly."

"That's a scary thought. Are you going to steal a plane to get some hours, you know, like you did with the C-17? And who are you going to fly for?"

"I don't have to steal anything, and I can fly right out of Redmond."

"You know, you can't keep that C-17. At some point you have to give it back to the government, along with all those Chinooks."

"You didn't let me finish. Do you know all of the carriers who fly out of Roberts Field in Redmond?"

"Podunk Airlines and maybe Podunkier Airlines?"

"Hardly. Redmond is the main airport serving all of Central Oregon. Did you know that at least eight passenger airlines fly out of here?"

"How do I know you're telling me the truth, Mr. Baker. Name them."

"Okay. Alaska, Allegiant, American Eagle, Avelo, Boutique, Delta Connection, and United. Besides those, there are at least two cargo carriers, AmeriFlight and Fedex."

"How do you know—"

"I'm not finished yet. Aerial firefighting aircraft owned by private companies fly out of here.

"In addition, the Forest Service flies out of here to fight forest fires. The United States Forest Service (USFS) Redmond Air Center is at the airport and supports regional firefighting operations and it provides training for smokejumper teams along with fuel, water, and fire retardant for the airtanker aircraft."

"What makes you think any of those will hire Radley Baker?"

"My military record, my record with the militia, and the recommendation of Colonel Craig ... maybe even a recommendation from Governor Harper."

***

As Shauna recounted the events of the past three or four weeks, it became apparent that even in the middle of all the chaos, Baker had been thinking about their future and what he would do to provide for them.

Even if he did a lot of *winging it*, Baker would take care of Shauna Jackson. He already had. And he would take care of Shauna Baker too.

"Yes."

"Yes? Munchkin, is that a nailed-down yes?"

She nodded. "I'll marry you as soon as that house is built."

"As soon as it's built? Is that a promise?"

"It's a promise."

Baker's smile seemed to twist into a smirk. What was he about to pull out of his sleeve?

Chapter 34

10:00 a.m., the next morning, Washington, DC, Oval Office

Wendell Walker sat alone at the Resolute Desk staring at his secure sat phone. Will Richards' meeting with the Joint Chiefs of Staff would last for at least another hour.

Should Walker place the call to General Wiley now, or wait for Will to join him in a conference call?

Since he had never revealed the details of this plan to his Secretary of Defense, Walker would tell Will later.

If Walker didn't bring Oregon under his control immediately, that state would stand as a symbol of victory for the resistance. That might mean the end of his presidency, if it hadn't ended already.

Strange rumors were running rampant and were even reported by some media outlets. Unverified sources said that America was making a hard right turn, going back to its Puritan roots, or some such nonsense.

Wendell Walker was still the Commander-in-Chief of the most powerful fighting force in the world. Surely, he could find one general who could get the job done in Oregon. But how could they do this job without air superiority?

After the Cold War ended and the air guard was given its current role in air defense, no one knew that the U.S. military would be fighting a ground war in the Pacific Northwest or else that move would never have been made. Regardless, it had left Walker without fighter interceptors in the Northwest and that had been disastrous.

Walker picked up his phone and keyed in the secure phone number for General Wiley, commander of a wing of

B-52s which had been practicing alert status in case that Cold War vestige needed to be resurrected. B-52s could drop B61 series nuclear bombs, making these bombers a likely candidate to be used in a modified nuclear dyad should ballistic missiles be decommissioned. And Walker wanted the ICBMs decommissioned. In his opinion, submarines were enough.

If he remembered correctly, B61's max warhead was over 300 kilotons, large enough to wipeout Washington, DC.

Wiley answered on the second ring. "General Wiley here."

"Wiley, this is President Walker. I need your help with a ticklish scenario."

"Yes, sir. Glad to help. What are the parameters?"

"First, how quickly can you bring up one B-52 on alert status with two B61 series nuclear bombs, the biggest we've got in the arsenal?"

"The biggest would be 340 kilotons, Mr. President. Since we've been practicing for just such a scenario, I would say six hours to get the bombs ready and two hours to arm the plane and put it on alert, ready to take off. If I am permitted to know, may I ask why you need this information?"

"Yes, you may. Do you have your maps app handy?"

"Bringing it up right now, Mr. President."

"Look at Central Oregon, the area around Redmond. How much damage would the two B61s do if one hit Crooked River Ranch and the other hit Redmond?"

"This is all hypothetical, right, sir?"

"Yes. Hypothetical."

"Well, Mr. President, you wouldn't need the second bomb. If one bomb hit Redmond, you would devastate an area from ... Madras on the north to Bend on the south. Crooked river Ranch and Redmond would be gone and everyone in the area I mentioned would die. With modern thermonuclear weapons, the fallout should degrade to habitable levels in about a year and a half ... are we expecting a nuclear attack?"

"No, Wiley. But the nation is facing an existential threat. The only way we can reunite the states and save the Union is to eliminate a powerful militia that is starting to slither across the nation from Oregon. We must cut off the serpent's head, or the United States will die a tortuous death."

"Sir, are we actually talking about bombing American citizens?"

"There's no other way, Wiley."

"This is insane, unconstitutional, and it violates the oath I took when I received my commission. Mr. President, I—"

"Wiley, need I remind you that—"

"Sir, you need remind me of nothing. I'm reminding **you** that if you convince another commander to carry out this plan, you will send this nation into a war bloodier and more destructive than what happened in 1861. Goodbye, Mr. President."

The explosion of adrenaline coursing through Walker's body nearly caused him to crush the sat phone he held in his right hand. He would have Wiley's stars if it was the last thing—

A sinking feeling doused the fire raging inside Walker. There was no one to help him. Whatever he did next might truly be the last thing he did as president and perhaps the last thing for Wendell Walker, the man.

Mr. President, how does it feel to be alone?

The mocking voice inside had stabbed his most vulnerable spot. Alone meant no military support while his enemies grew like a metastatic malignancy across the nation. And there was now no way to excise the malignancy or drive it into remission.

For the first time since taking office, Walker was truly alone.

He stood and wandered toward his private study, unable to string coherent thoughts together. His thoughts had turned to urges, urges driving him to perform unthinkable actions.

Walker entered the study and locked the door.

Before he could reach the chair behind his desk, an anapestic knock sounded on the door.

Will Richards. Walker's most trusted ally in his administration and his last hope for a way out of defeat and the despair it brought.

He unlocked the door and hurried to take his seat. "Come in, Will."

How much and how quickly should he unload his burden on Will Richards?

Will stopped in front of his desk but didn't take his usual seat. "Mr. President, I've got some news that you need to hear."

The tone of his voice said this was not good news. Will seldom panicked, but he sounded like he was on the verge.

"Did you know that the congressional leaders of both houses have been meeting remotely?"

"No. I thought they were afraid to come to DC and that they were all busy taking care of their families, especially those living in large cities."

"They have drafted and tentatively agreed—both houses—on charges against you and incorporated them into articles of impeachment."

So the nation found some common ground to reunite, the demise of President Wendell Walker.

Will continued, "I surmised you might try using the military to regain control. If you do, you will fail."

"What do you mean?"

"I called all of my trusted contacts, generals and other commanders of large organizations that you might try to use. I haven't been able to find one commander that will take orders from you. Mr. President, you are a walking, talking violation of the Constitution, that document I swore to protect."

"What are you saying, Will?"

"Let me tell it to you plain. You're going down, Walker. I tried to warn you that this might be the consequences if you kept pushing toward absolute control. But you didn't listen, so I now must testify against you."

"You too, Will? But I still have the support of a large percentage of the population."

"Only in some of the big metropolitan areas. And even on the military bases near the big cities, you don't have any support. Face it, Wendell. You will be impeached, tried, and almost certainly found guilty on multiple charges. You will be removed from office and—"

"But that's all they can do to me. Remove me from the presidency."

"I wasn't finished, sir. I was about to say, heaven only knows how far Congress will go in trying to prosecute you for your crimes. You killed American citizens with black military operations and attempted to kill several more."

He wouldn't tell Will that he also planned to nuke the Central Oregon Militia. But Wiley could testify to that. The walls seemed to be closing in on President Wendell Walker.

"Sir, the rest of your cabinet has already emptied out their offices and left. I have to consider my family. I'm leaving too." Will turned and walked out, closing the door behind him.

Despite some Secret Service agents and a few administrative staff still in the White House complex, Walker was completely alone. And when news that impeachment proceedings had begun reached the media, most of the population would turn against him. Eventually, Wiley would talk and then Walker's circumstances would turn dire.

Wendell Walker could let this situation end on their terms or his own. He had made too many mistakes and that put him in this impossible situation. The first mistake was not sending a strong army in when he first heard about Colonel David Craig and his militia.

Regardless, Craig would not get the chance to do what he had done nine years ago, enter the West Wing and arrest the President of the United States.

Like Reagan had done after the assassination attempt, Walker carried a gun. It drove the Secret Service wild, but President Reagan had set a precedent and Walker had used it.

He reached under the back of his suit jacket and curled his fingers around the grip of the Glock. He had always assumed he might use this weapon to thwart an assassination, but never an impeachment.

The gun slid easily from the holster.

He took a deep breath and let it out slowly, but that did not stop his hand from shaking.

Walker raised the gun to his temple.

A fleeting thought ran through his mind.

Does anything come after this? Anything at all.

You're about to find out, Mr. President.

The sarcastic remark that seemed to come from a demonic voice inside his mind angered him. Walker squeezed hard on the trigger.

Chapter 35

11:30 a.m., the same day, Terrebonne, Oregon

Craig and Susan met for their lunch date at the Pump House in Terrebonne. He sat around the corner of the table from Susan. It was a warm sunny day, so they had chosen a table outside on the deck, and they sat under the shade of a big blue and white umbrella.

With only two weeks until their wedding, he and Susan still had one major decision to make. Where were they going to live?

Susan studied his face for a moment. "The issue has been resolved."

"What do you mean?"

"We only had one big issue left hanging, where we were going to live starting in about two weeks."

"And that's resolved without my input?"

She reached across the corner of the table and took his hand. "I bet that I could convince you that I'm right."

One look into her bright blue eyes set in a perfectly sculpted face would be enough to convince any red-blooded male of anything she argued for.

"We're going to live in my house."

"But what about your mom, Susan?"

"She enjoyed spending the past few months with me, but she misses her friends and her church back in Prineville."

"Is this her idea?"

"A few days ago, she told me she was moving. I waited to be sure that it was what she really wanted. It is. She was only waiting for the conflict to end and to be sure a certain colonel was not going to leave me at the altar."

"This colonel would never let a woman like you get away if he could help it."

"But mom remembers what happened to me when one man did."

"Not gonna happen, Susan. Do you want me to tell her?"

"No. Both mom and I understand that."

"Good."

"But what are you going to do with your big motorhome?"

"Correction. *Our* big motorhome. We're going to travel in it, wherever your heart desires."

"What will you do, David? You never got paid to command the militia and soon you won't even have that to do."

"If it's our income you're concerned about, I have a decent retirement from the military and a lot of years of savings from the many times the army stationed me in places where I couldn't spend my pay."

"I have some savings too. And the money from the sale of Crooked River Espresso to Kate. But do you think we can count on our savings and investments with the nation still so fragmented?"

"Yes, we can count on our savings and investments. The economy and the banking system haven't gone too far to recover. We should be okay provided nothing else happens to stop the unification of the country. But remember, it's God who's putting the nation back together."

She smiled. "I guess He's not done with America yet."

"And that being the case, we don't have to work. If we choose to work, we don't have to earn a big salary to survive. That leaves us free to travel."

Craig's phone rang.

He glanced at the caller ID. "It's Zach. He's at the radio station today. I'd better take it. He might have some important news."

"Craig here."

"Craig, have you listened to any news over the last couple of hours?"

"No. What's up?"

"President Walker committed suicide earlier today."

Craig weighed Zach's words for what seemed like minutes before replying. "What about the vice president?"

"She resigned and left town. How do you read this, Craig, and what should we do?"

Craig turned on the speakerphone. "Slide your chair next to mine, Susan. You'll want to hear this. The president committed suicide."

"Oh, my goodness." She scooted closer to Craig.

"Here are my first thoughts on this, Zach. We'll need to call a meeting of the militia leaders so we're all in sync. But this is a complete, irrevocable, and unconditional surrender by Walker. He knew he had no chance of winning any war that he tried to wage. That and the spiritual movement sweeping the nation will bring a measure of unity we haven't seen in a long time."

"But what about the state of the nation in the short-term?" Zach asked.

"There will be political instability for the next few days, but the Speaker of the House, a strong constitutionalist, will be sworn in as president. As he takes over and starts making wise decisions, which I'm confident he will do, things will settle down."

"What about the military? Should we worry about further attacks?"

"No. We'll remain prepared, but the U.S. military will fall in line under the new president. They disliked Walker anyway." Craig paused. "It's not a good thing to lose an

American president for any reason, but I do believe Walker was correct. He could not win. That must have plunged him into a hopelessness he couldn't deal with."

"Between a rock and a hard place," Zach said.

Susan sighed. "Or between **the Rock** and a hot place."

"You got that right," Zach said.

"I'll call Steve and Julia to make arrangements for a meeting at their place tonight. Since Sandra went back to Salem, I'm going to see if we can patch her into the meeting via video. We need a coordinated posture between the Guard and the militia for the next few weeks. Can you be there, Zach?"

"I'll try to be there, sir."

"For security reasons, won't you need to monitor the political and the people's responses across the nation, especially in the Northwest?" Susan said.

"Yes. That requires you and the gang at Crooked River Espresso to be pumping every traveler who comes through for information we might need. Sandra is officially the Guard commander, so I'll ask her to contact them and keep us posted on what the Guard response will be and what their intelligence officers are hearing."

"Sir, do you think there might be any leftist lunatics out there who will try to retaliate?"

"I don't know, Zach. That's why we need to remain vigilant until most of the dust settles. We'll talk about that tonight."

"See you tonight, sir." Zach dropped off the call.

Craig locked his phone.

"Is the fighting over, David?" Susan had lowered her voice to that tone she used for their most intimate conversations. "After the close calls we all had, I can't stand the thought of you being in danger again."

"My gut tells me the combat is over. But we won't disband the militia until the political battles have been won.

Politics. That's where we need God to call more leaders to repentance, especially leaders from the left. That would have a huge impact on this nation," he said. "For now, we remain prepared, we watch, and we wait."

Susan took his free hand. "Yes, we wait for two more weeks."

When Susan smiled like that, Craig wondered how any fool could have left this woman at the altar.

Chapter 36

Later the same afternoon

The big engine in his Trackhawk rumbled as Baker slowed and pulled into the circle drive in front of Julia's big house. He stopped near the front porch.

Drew's, Brock's, Craig's, and Lex's vehicles were already parked ahead of him.

By the time Baker turned off the engine, Shauna stood on the porch with her arms folded across her petite, perfectly formed body.

"You're late, Baker."

Was that a good thing or a bad thing?

This visit was supposed to be a surprise. Had she been watching for him to drive up Chinook Drive on the ranch plateau below? If so, she must have been out on the Bancrofts' deck. But why?

Her folded arms, other body posture, and the look of displeasure on her face said it was a bad thing.

He knew better than to spit in the spitfire's eye. That could earn a person a black eye and an unpleasant monologue. But he had to say something. "Got a question for you."

"Didn't I already answer your most important question?" She gave him that Mona Lisa smile that hid whatever was going on behind those large, lustrous brown eyes.

He'd take that smile, though it was demurring. "Then maybe this question is only the second most important."

Shauna stepped close enough to clasp her hands behind his neck. "Ask me then."

This was progress. "Well, Zach and Kate are getting married this weekend, then Craig's and Susan's wedding is two weeks after that."

She nodded, turned her head to one side, and eyed him from the corner of her big brown eyes."

"You said, quote, 'I'll marry you as soon as the house is built.' I'm here to inform you, Munchkin, the house is built."

Shauna took a step back. "Baker, this morning I drove by that lot you bought, and there's no house sitting there. What do you take me for?"

"I take you for *me*, Munchkin. That's all I've wanted since the day I met you."

"Nice try. Now where's the house?"

"If you'd just let me explain instead of always trying—"

"*Always*? That's a word you should *always* avoid. It's *never* the truth. And *never's* a word you should *never* use in an argument."

"But you used—"

"I'm busy, Baker. You'll have to find some other time for me to ignore you, muscle-bound meathead."

What was that about?

Steve stepped out of his house and stopped behind Shauna. "Ouch. Baker, are you going to just stand there and let her insult you like that?"

Shauna turned and flashed Steve a dagger-like glance. "That wasn't an insult. It was a description."

Steve chuckled.

"Sorry for bothering you, Shauna," Baker said. "I forgot that I only exist when you need me for something really important, like saving your life."

"If you were the only muscle-bound meathead of a man on the planet, maybe I wouldn't want to live. Maybe I would end it all—just climb to the top of your ego, dive off, and splatter all over your IQ."

Steve's chuckle turned to a guffaw. "You'd better quit before it gets worse, Baker. When things get that bad between you and a girl, there's only one thing you can do."

He shot Steve a sharp glance. "Okay, funny guy. What's that ... as if I'm really interested in your opinion."

"Even a meathead like you should be able to figure it out." Steve waved Baker toward Shauna.

After he had moved to within an arm's reach of Shauna, he gripped both of her shoulders.

"Don't you dare, Baker."

"What happened to meathead?"

She didn't reply.

Baker pulled her closer.

She didn't resist.

He kissed her.

She let him. First it was unconditional surrender, then she joined his side in the skirmish.

After the incredible moment ended, Shauna pressed her cheek into Baker's chest. "I'm sorry. I didn't mean all of that."

He smiled down at her. "Maybe you can be sorry again sometime soon."

She slipped from his arms and stepped back. "Or maybe not, Runt."

"Meathead to runt. At least I'm coming up in the world."

"No. You're—"

He pressed his fingers over her mouth. "It's my turn to talk, sweetheart."

"Okay. Explain the house."

"The house that's built is a manufactured home sitting on a lot in Woodburn, Oregon."

"Oh, how wonderful. A trailer house. An Oklahoma tornado magnet."

"Shauna, it's a very nice eighteen-hundred-square-foot home that we will live in until our dream house is built. You see, I had some savings from my re-enlistment bonuses and other savings from my time in Afghanistan—four years in a dusty country where there's no place to spend money."

"And our dream house?"

"It will be built carefully, as you and I design it together, while we enjoy marital bliss in our brand new home, starting two weeks after Craig's and Susan's wedding."

"You're asking me to marry you in four weeks? Why didn't you say so?"

"Because you wouldn't let me say anything."

"I was miffed because I thought you were stalling about setting the date. You know, once you get off dead center, you're a fast mover, Radley Baker."

"Gotta be fast if you want to steal C-17s and such."

Baker looked over Shauna's shoulder at Steve's tall figure. "Steve, you can get lost now."

"But this is much more interesting than the conversation Julia and I were having."

"Glad you enjoyed it. Now, dude, will you kindly disappear?"

Steve turned to go back inside. "Just when it was getting really interesting. Marital bliss."

The door closed.

"There's more I wanted to tell you, Munchkin."

"This isn't a good news, bad news thing, is it?"

He gave her his warmest smile, hoping he hadn't lit another fuse in her bewildering arsenal of emotions. "You told me your mom and dad planned to retire in about four years. How would they like to have a nice little eighteen-hundred-square-foot mother-in-law cottage on the corner of our property as a retirement gift, a place to live out their golden years?"

"You need to meet them, Baker. Especially if we're tying the knot in four weeks. So you can ask them yourself." She pressed her cheek against his chest.

Shauna was listening to his heartbeat.

It was beating rather fast.

The door opened again, and Steve stuck his head out. "I hate to interrupt, but Zach's show is starting, and he said he has some important news."

"I suppose we should go in," Shauna said.

He kissed her forehead. "Yeah. We've got some important news to tell them too."

Nearly the whole gang sat in the great room when Baker and Shauna walked in. Even Kathy and Itzy were there.

"Is Kate here," Shauna asked.

"Nope." Steve turned up the audio and Kate's alto voice came through the sound system.

"And that's why not even an ideological war could permanently come between Aunt Sandy and me."

"It was a war I was destined to lose, with you and Jesus against me." Governor Harper's voice.

"And now Dad is attending an Alpha group meeting. He says he enjoys it. And he will be here at the Ranch Chapel to give me away next week."

"And Laura, my little sister ..." Sandra said, "... though still the skeptic, might join him at the next meeting."

"Reconciliation." Zach said. "That's what Christianity is all about—horizontally, but most of all vertically." He paused. "And what about reconciliation across this nation, Governor?"

"As you know, the awakening has swept through nearly every state. It has taken in some of the political leadership. Now we have a strong basis for uniting these divided states. We still have a way to go, but the way has been prepared by what transpired in this little West Coast state that I have the honor of representing."

Sandra continued. "Oregonians, actually all Americans, owe Colonel David Craig a deep debt of gratitude, and from what I have heard from the president, perhaps we owe him another medal of honor."

"There you have it, folks," Zach said. "As someone once said, 'With God on our side, we will find a way to stitch this riven republic together again, because He's a good God. He blessed America before, and He can do it again.'"

The End

If you enjoyed *Restored*, please consider leaving a rating and a brief review on Amazon. Reviews are difficult to get and greatly appreciated by authors and readers. You can find *Restored* and all my other novels on H. L. Wegley's Amazon Author Page.

Author's Notes

The Skylight Cave—not again!

Sorry, but I couldn't help myself for several reasons. First, the cave is a natural wonder with many potential hazards for thriller-level action scenes. Second, Julia Bancroft had a life changing experience here in my novel _Voice of Freedom_. The cave is where she lost her pacifistic beliefs after realizing that in this fallen world, we must defend ourselves and our loved ones from evil, even if that requires the use of deadly force. Third, drawing from Julia's story, the cave was the logical place that a vengeful brother, Nicholas Deke, would choose to kill Julia.

Nature of the Divisions in America

The _Riven Republic Series_ portrays America dividing over ideological differences, the constitutionalists on the right against the growing force of Marxism on the left.

Politically, I suppose this division is true and it makes national reconciliation difficult. But at a deeper level, this division goes to the roots of what constitutionalists believe, _i.e._ theism and more specifically the Judeo-Christian morality and ethics. These beliefs are pitted against the roots of Marxism, which include atheism and egregious violations of biblical morality, ethics, and the honoring of our Maker, Almighty God.

Constitutionalists adhering to Judeo-Christian beliefs, which are the foundation of America, against Marxism, is essentially a war between good and evil. This is a conflict that will never be resolved in this age. That's why hope for unity in America is increasingly focusing on revival in America, a movement of God across our land as in the Great Awakening and the two other major movements of God that occurred later.

Why does that notion, a war of good against evil requiring God's involvement, cause such rage on the left?

Well, the following is some background that should answer that question.

If you read recent U.S. history books, you will find very little about Christianity except statements that paint it in a bad light. So I scanned older U.S. history texts dating back to 1922, and I was surprised that I found very little about religion's role in the founding of our nation. The bit of information mentioned was both sketchy and non-representative of what most American citizens intuitively believe.

Skipping the history texts, let's simply look at a Supreme Court Case from 1892 and see how SCOTUS viewed the religious roots of America. Supreme Court Justice David Brewer delivered the court's opinion below:

U.S. Supreme Court 1892
Church of the Holy Trinity v. United States, Page 143 U.S. 457 (1892)

There is no dissonance in these declarations [U.S. Constitution and State Constitutions]. There is a universal language pervading them all, having one meaning. They affirm and reaffirm that this is a religious nation. These are not individual sayings, declarations of private persons. They are organic utterances. They speak the voice of the entire people ...

"Christianity, general Christianity, is, and always has been, a part of the common law of Pennsylvania; . . . not Christianity with an established church and tithes and spiritual courts, but Christianity with liberty of conscience to all men ..."

"But, beyond all these matters, no purpose of action against religion can be imputed to any legislation, state or national, because this is a religious people. This is historically true. From the discovery of this continent to the present hour, there is a single voice making this affirmation ...

"These, and many other matters which might be noticed, add a volume of unofficial declarations to the mass of organic utterances that *this is a Christian nation*." https://supreme.justia.com/cases/federal/us/143/457/

That statement, like a lightning rod, divides the passionately patriotic Americans from those easily led to hold other opinions. At the far end of the *easily led* are the Marxists who are making inroads to destroy everything of value in America, everything that made this nation great and good. Their immediate goal is to destroy our culture, our history, morality, the nuclear family, our economy, our churches, and our unity—divide and conquer by making us think that none of what used to make sense makes sense anymore.

We must not let these followers of the demonized man, Karl Marx, divide us, feed us a counterfeit history of America, or feed us nonsense about the most disastrous, murderous, boneheaded political system in the history of mankind. When we contemplate the hundreds of millions of people Marx's ideas have slaughtered, it is no stretch to believe this destructive form of government came straight from the one who seeks to steal, kill, and destroy, i.e. Satan himself. That should not be surprising when we consider that many of Marx's contemporaries considered him a demonized Satan worshiper.

Here's some evidence to further establish the depravity of Karl Marx. He was a deadbeat who wouldn't work, so four of his children died of malnutrition before reaching adulthood. He was a racist who hated Africans. Marx abused his wife, was unfaithful, fathering a child out of wedlock. He was a filthy man who did not bathe. That beard you see in his portraits—there be dragons in there! He was such a troublemaker he was kicked out of three countries.

There's a lot more that could be added to this list. But what I've already listed begs the question, "Why would anyone follow the ideas created by such a man?" Man's fallen nature evidently seduces him to follow Karl Marx even though Marx's ideas have killed at least 200 million people.

Problems with Featuring a Large Cast

I can't end my notes on such a downer, so I'll mention my cast of militia warfighters and their spouses. This group of exceptional people, drawn from my previous novels that were set in Central Oregon, gave me a cast of characters that proved to be overwhelming. How do you feature fourteen or fifteen characters in a single series, each of which could, at any moment, steal the show? The struggle to let them all fill a meaningful role created many headaches for me and contributed to the delay in releasing book 3 of the series.

Also. I also had to keep room open for the new heroes and heroines, Kate and Zach, Craig and Susan, and Shauna and Baker. I hope you enjoyed the result of the many compromises I made to include all these folks into the *Riven Republic Series*.

So long until my next story, a thriller partly ripped from the headlines and partly pulled from cancelled sources that never made it to the headlines in our highly censored world of would-be Marxist revolutionaries.

H. L. Wegley

Discussion Questions

1. Late in the story, when Baker pops the question to Shauna and starts iterating through the issues that might make her say no, he mentions the race issue. He's half Modoc and Shauna is an African American. What do you think about Shauna's answer to Baker's concern about a mixed marriage? Here are Shauna's words. "Baker, every marriage is a mixed marriage—two different people raised in two different families often in different parts of the country. It's always a challenge, especially if people aren't committed to God and to His institution of marriage **before** they commit to each other."

2. What did you think about Shauna's charge to Zach to call the nation to repentance? How badly is this needed today? What would you add to her list of American sins in Chapter 2? What would you remove from it?

3. In the author's notes, I referenced a Supreme Court case from 1892 where the SCOTUS justice presenting the court's opinion gave evidence for American being a Christian nation. Do you agree with the court's rationale? Do you think America is a Christian nation or ever was such a nation?

4. Colonel Craig's internal monologue: "The carnage was widespread and sickening, especially to realize they were doing this to American troops. And knowing that these troops were following unconstitutional orders didn't help the sick feeling in his gut." Do you believe Craig was justified in killing fellow Americans who were following the president's unconstitutional orders to kill Craig and his men? Keep in mind that a soldier's oath of enlistment or of office is to defend the Constitution.

5. If you read the entire *Riven Republic Series*, you have seen Sandra Harper gradually turn from her radical left political ideology, largely due to her love for her niece, Kate. And Kate never stopped loving her aunt, though Aunt Sandie tried to break up her relationship with Zach, split her church using lies, and even tried to kidnap Kate to deprogram her and return her to their powerful political family. Have you seen love-based relationships bring people to faith in Christ? How important are relationships when trying to reach people whose worldview is much different than yours?

6. Shauna's small size and her life experiences, such as people getting hurt when she tried to help them, made her think that she was inferior, a person who always came up short. How did Baker help her realize that she wasn't inferior, that she was a person of incredible worth? Is there anything you can learn from Baker's example to help someone you know who feels they have no value?

7. Baker's scheme to steal a C-17, a plane he had minimal experience with, and use it to evacuate the women and children before they could be attacked seems foolhardy. Here's what Baker said about it. "I cooked up this scheme because we need to protect our families. Sure it's challenging, but God would have shown me another way if this was foolhardy." How do we decide when to discourage people from doing things we think are foolish? Is the rationale that Baker used sound biblical reasoning, or was he being a fool?

8. What role(s) might you play in calling America back to God? What would you have to do to prepare for that role? When do you intend to get started?

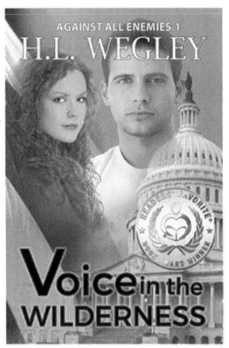

Don't miss H. L.Wegley's award-winning, political-thriller series, with romance, *Against All Enemies*:

Book 1: Voice in the Wilderness

Book 2: Voice of Freedom

Book 3: Chasing Freedom (The Prequel)

Read all three books in the *Witness Protection Series*—action and romance with thriller-level stakes—clean reads that are never graphic, gratuitous, or gross.

This series can be read in any order.

No Turning Back

When a young man much like her father offers her protection, will trusting him bring another massacre, one that takes her life too?

Witness Protection Series

Book 1: No Safe Place

Book 2: No True Justice

Book 3: No Turning Back

Read all three books in the *Riven Republic Series*—thriller-level stakes in a divided America. See what a modern-day civil war might look like and what it would take to bring America back to *e pluribus unum.*

1. <u>Riven</u>
2. <u>Resisting</u>
3. <u>Restored</u>

Silver Medal, 2021 Readers' Favorites Book Awards

When her father is murdered, he left her with a warning, an assassin on her trail, and his secret history contained in a set of journals. As Allie tries to elude the assassin and read the journals, she learns that the loving father who raised her was not the man he appeared to be, and the man she must now trust with her life is someone Allie must never trust with her heart.

At strong safety, Grady Jamison could defend against opponents in the red zone, but he couldn't stop the drunk driver who hit his car and killed his sister. Does Allie Petrenko's call for help mean Grady has been given a second chance, a chance to do things right?

The Janus Journals, an epic, dual timeline story of story of love, courage, forgiveness and faith.

Romantic suspense with thriller-level stakes

Vince van Gordon inherits control of break-through, virtual-reality technology that could make him one of the wealthiest and most powerful people on the planet. But, if commercialized, the technology would likely shred the fabric of American society beyond mending. Keeping it a secret only delays the inevitable. And, once the secret is leaked, there are people who will kill for the wealth and power. Stopping it may literally require an Act of Congress, and Vince will need the help of brilliant Jess Jamison, his childhood soulmate, the girl who shattered his heart seven years ago.

Bronze Medal, 2019 Readers' Favorites Book Awards

Virtuality

Made in the USA
Middletown, DE
17 September 2021